Keep Holding On

Also by

Susane Colasanti

When It Happens
Take Me There
Waiting for You
Something Like Fate
So Much Closer

Keep Holding On

SUSANE COLASANTI

VIKING

An Imprint of Penguin Group (USA) Inc.

VIKING
Published by Penguin Group
Penguin Young Readers Group, 345 Hudson Street, New York, New York 10014, U.S.A.
Penguin Group (Canada), 90 Eglinton Avenue East, Suite 700, Toronto, Ontario, Canada M4P 2Y3
(a division of Pearson Penguin Canada Inc.)
Penguin Books Ltd, 80 Strand, London WC2R 0RL, England
Penguin Ireland, 25 St Stephen's Green, Dublin 2, Ireland (a division of Penguin Books Ltd)
Penguin Group (Australia), 250 Camberwell Road, Camberwell, Victoria 3124, Australia
(a division of Pearson Australia Group Pty Ltd)
Penguin Books India Pvt Ltd, 11 Community Centre, Panchsheel Park, New Delhi—110 017, India
Penguin Group (NZ), 67 Apollo Drive, Rosedale, Auckland 0632, New Zealand
(a division of Pearson New Zealand Ltd.)
Penguin Books (South Africa) (Pty) Ltd, 24 Sturdee Avenue, Rosebank, Johannesburg 2196,
South Africa
Penguin Books Ltd, Registered Offices: 80 Strand, London WC2R 0RL, England
First published in 2012 by Viking, a division of Penguin Young Readers Group

1   3   5   7   9   10   8   6   4   2

Copyright © Susane Colasanti, 2012

LIBRARY OF CONGRESS CATALOGING-IN-PUBLICATION DATA
Colasanti, Susane.
Keep holding on / by Susane Colasanti.
p. cm.
Summary: Bullied at school and neglected by her poor, self-absorbed, single mother at home, high
school junior Noelle finally reaches the breaking point after a classmate commits suicide.
ISBN 978-0-670-01225-1 (hardcover)
[1. Self-perception—Fiction. 2. Bullies—Fiction. 3. Poverty—Fiction. 4. High schools—
Fiction. 5. Schools—Fiction.] I. Title.
PZ7.C6699Ke 2012
[Fic]—dc23
2011028232

Printed in U.S.A.   Set in Minion

PEARSON

For Tyler Clementi.

For every other teen who felt like
they couldn't hold on anymore.

And for everyone who's been bullied,
neglected, or left out.

You are not alone.
Be strong and never give up.

Keep
Holding
On

one

tuesday, april 5

(53 days left)

Julian Porter is blocking me.

The blocking is probably unintentional. He sits two rows behind me in Spanish. We have to use the same aisle to get to our desks. I know he's already been to his desk because his notebook and pen are sitting on it. Maybe he forgot something in his locker. Whatever the reason, he's coming out of our aisle as I'm trying to go in.

Julian moves over to let me pass. I can feel him smiling down at me, but I can't really look up at him. Looking at him is beyond intense. It's like looking at the sun. But I can see him without looking. Images of Julian are burned into my brain. Hazel-green eyes. Disheveled sandy-blond hair. All-American Boy build. Four inches taller than me. Even the intricacies of his glasses are permanently etched in my memory, with their rectangular black frames that glint electric blue when the light catches them a certain way.

I press up against Julian as I brush past him. We're talking serious sensory overload here. I'm overwhelmed with more attraction in this instant than I've ever felt with Matt Brennan. And I let Matt put his hands all over me.

I want Julian Porter to put his hands all over me. I want him to take me to his room and kiss me all night.

Does liking two boys at the same time make me a slut?

Having Spanish with Julian is excruciating. I'm always wondering if he's looking at me. Or at least thinking about me. When I'm supposed to be paying attention to imperfect verb conjugation, I'm sneaking looks at Julian instead. There are ways to sneak looks at him without being obvious. Usually, I pretend I'm looking at something to the side and then rely on my peripheral vision. Or I'll turn around and pretend to be interested when someone in the back is answering a question. I don't like watching people answer questions, though. I get so nervous when teachers call on me. And the way everyone stares at me when I'm answering makes me even more nervous.

The bell rings for class to start. Julian comes back to our aisle. My heart pounds so hard I suspect it's visible to anyone within a five-mile radius. On his way back to his desk, Julian slides two fingers over the fresh page in my notebook.

Why did he touch my notebook like that?

What does it mean?

I have a sudden urge to rip out the page and save it. But if Julian saw me do that, it would be crazy obvious. I might be crazy obvious when I sneak looks at him, too. I should probably cut down on that.

◆ ◆ ◆

No one ever wants to sit with me at lunch.

I never look around in the cafeteria. Being forced to sit here like some trapped zoo animal eating alone for the whole world to watch is embarrassing enough. I really don't need to see them laughing at me.

I wish I could be transported to another school in an alternate universe where required learning doesn't have to involve this traumatic test of survival skills. No one would care if you're different in the alternate universe. Or maybe *everyone* would be different. How cool would it be if differences were celebrated? And the more different you were, the better? Fitting in would be a totally foreign concept.

But no. I'm stuck in this universe.

Chew.

Swallow.

Chew.

Swallow.

Don't look up.

Tommy sits alone at the small table by the door. I sneak a glance at him. Our eyes lock.

The Eye Lock says, *We are both outsiders.*

We are outsiders for different reasons. Tommy doesn't fit in due to extreme geekitude. With me, it's a lot more complicated.

I look back down at my lunch. Tommy and I have acknowledged that we are both rejects. But each of us will continue to pretend that we're not the bigger reject.

My lunch is:

- sandwich consisting of white bread, lettuce, and mayo
- some store-brand potato chips
- water

I qualify for free lunch, but there's no way I'd subject myself to that kind of humiliation. You have to show a special card that everyone would see. The free-lunch cards are orange. The normal cards are blue. I'd rather scavenge in our empty refrigerator than have everyone know how poor I am.

Not that I'd ever buy lunch anyway. Back when I had friends, I might have gone up to get a pack of cookies or something. But now I'd have to walk all the way from the front of the cafeteria to my table in the back with everyone watching. Which would draw even more attention to the fact that I sit alone.

There's a snort of laughter from the next table. My shoulders clench.

Warner Talbot is pointing at my sandwich. I try to avoid sitting near him. But when you're the person no one wants to sit with, you don't always have a choice about where you end up.

"Dude," Warner says. "Her sandwich is only lettuce!"

"That's messed up," someone at his table says.

My face burns.

Their sandwiches are fat with meat and cheese and lettuce and tomato. I bet those cold cuts are the expensive ones from the deli section at the gourmet grocery store. I bet their sandwiches have two kinds of cheese. I try to imagine what it feels like to bite into a sandwich packed with all those things. Crunching through the lettuce. The juicy tomato bursting with flavor. The soft succulence of the meat and cheese.

Rich-kid sandwiches must taste incredible.

I try to hide my sad sandwich under the table. That just makes them laugh harder.

Making fun of me apparently never gets old for Warner Talbot. He's been exposing my lunches for two years, ever since the first day of ninth grade. All I could find in the refrigerator that day was mayonnaise, mustard, and the end slice of some bread. So I made a mayonnaise and mustard sandwich. Well, half a sandwich—I had to fold the slice of bread over. And somehow, Warner was right there laughing at me. It was like his radar for unfortunate people went ballistic when it detected me, all flashing red lights and wailing sirens.

Warner says, "Someone throw this girl a biscuit."

Everyone at his table laughs.

They know I can hear them.

They just don't care.

◆　◆　◆

My last class is precalc. The anticipation of freedom in forty-six minutes almost makes me like math.

I dart to my desk in the second row. I'd much rather sit in the back. But I had to move up this year. Some of the things teachers were writing on the board were starting to look blurry.

These two rowdy boys who sit in the back bust in right as the bell rings. They're wearing almost identical polo shirts. Everyone dresses the same around here. Everything is The Same. All of the big suburban houses are practically identical, with their saccharine front yards and indistinguishable driveways and uninspired architectural designs. People in this town hate anything different. No one is allowed to diverge from conformity. Original thoughts, interests, and style choices are strictly prohibited. And if you disobey these rules? There are consequences.

My town is like thousands of other American towns. You might have heard of it: Middle of Nowhere, USA.

Welcome to suburban wasteland.

As if subsisting in a town that's ultra conventional and entirely devoid of culture weren't enough fun times, this is the kind of suburbia that borders on the country. So it's remote enough not to be close to anything interesting. The city is an hour away. Which might as well be twenty hours away without a car. If I had a car, I could escape this hateful town whenever I wanted. I'd drive to the city every day after school and stay until it got late.

I don't know why we live here. We don't even remotely fit in. We rent the second floor of a little, dilapidated house from an old lady who's lived here forever. The carpet, kitchen appliances, and wallpaper didn't get the memo that 1964 is ancient history. Newer, bigger houses have gone up all around this one.

I cannot wait to leave this place and never look back. Maybe I'll live in the city. Or in another city even farther away. I don't want to see any of these people ever again. Except Sherae. I'm lucky to have a good friend. She hates how cookie-cutter everything is around here, too.

Every day is a countdown to graduation. That day I'm set free will be the Best Day Ever. The calendar on my wall has a countdown to the end of the year. I did the same thing last year. Next year will be the last one.

I want to help make the world a better place when I am far away from here. Because if we're not improving the world in some way, then what's the point?

Things will get better after this.

They have to.

two

thursday, april 7

(51 days left)

Sherae is still having nightmares.

"I've been up since four," she says. She looks even more exhausted than she sounds.

"I wish there was something I could do," I tell her. I'd do anything to take her pain away. But I wouldn't even know how to begin saying the right things to her.

Sherae is staring into her locker like she forgot what she was looking for.

"Maybe I should have told someone," she says.

I definitely think she should have told someone. I really wanted her to. But Sherae just wanted to forget about it and move on.

I'm still hoping she'll change her mind.

◆　◆　◆

Graffiti in the second-floor girls' bathroom, written in black marker on the wall above the first sink:

Noelle Wexler Is Corroded

• • •

There's this thing I do with Matt Brennan. It's a secret thing. Something Matt said I can never tell anyone. I really want to tell Sherae. But I promised him I wouldn't.

Matt Brennan and I make out.

We sneak away when we're supposed to be in study hall. Not every day. Just a few times a week. It's not like we're missing anything. And the monitor is so spotty about taking attendance that we usually aren't even marked absent. We meet behind the stone wall across from the tennis courts. No one ever goes back there. It's not a nice place to hang out. It's just a scraggly patch in the middle of some trees. There's nowhere to sit. It gets muddy when it rains. But it's good for making out. And when I'm kissing Matt, I can block out everything else.

Matt has a bad-boy reputation. But just because someone always wears a black motorcycle jacket and looks angry most of the time doesn't mean he's trouble. I heard he was into some hard-core stuff like dealing drugs, but he told me those are just rumors. Only, Matt also told me that his parents suspended his allowance, and that's why he's working at the gas station. He wouldn't tell me why he got in trouble. Even though we're close physically, there's this distance between us that never seems to go away.

We don't say much when we get together at our place. We just start kissing. We haven't started kissing today, though. I'm still mad about what happened last week.

"I said I was sorry," Matt reminds me. "What else do you want?"

"Um, I don't know. Not to be your dirty little secret anymore?"

Matt puts his arms around me. He hugs me close.

"You know it's not like that," he whispers.

I want to believe him. I really, really do. But he didn't even tell me it was his birthday last week. I had to find out from overhearing his friends talk about his party. Which I wasn't invited to.

"Are you embarrassed to be seen with me?" I ask.

"No!"

"Then why can't we go out and do things like normal people?" I push away from him. This isn't how a boyfriend is supposed to act after you've been together for a whole month. Matt should want us to hang out with his friends. He should want to take me places. But I can't give up on him. I'm lucky to have him. And I know he can change.

"You want to go somewhere?" Matt says.

"Yes."

"Fine, we'll go somewhere."

"When?"

"Next Friday. Okay?"

"Okay."

Then Matt starts kissing me. I forget all about the birthday present for him in my bag.

◆ ◆ ◆

I have Spanish right before lunch. My stomach always growls in class. When I feel a growl coming on, I'll do something like cough or flip pages loudly to hide it. It's so obvious what I'm doing, though. The worst is when we're taking a test and we have to be quiet for the whole period. I get so nervous that my stomach's going to growl. Which of course makes it start growling.

The fact that Julian can hear my stomach growling makes me want to run away and never come back.

Luckily, it's a very noisy day in Spanish. Mrs. Yuknis started the class by playing some music. Then she pointed to where the music came from on the South America/Spain combo map. George asked if the music was going to be on the test.

At the beginning of the year, everyone was assigned a Spanish name. Noelle doesn't translate to anything, so I got Belén. Julian is Julio. Anything's better than what George got. He has to be Jorge. Which sucks for him because it's pronounced "whore-hey."

"*Entonces*," Mrs. Yuknis says. Then she says a bunch of other stuff in Spanish. I'm totally lost. I know I should know what she's saying by now. But I'm still clueless most of the time.

Mrs. Yuknis is wearing the same pants she wore on Monday. She's done this Monday/Thursday wearing-of-the-same-pants thing before. When the pants make their second appearance of the week, they are considerably more wrinkled. Does she not know we know? Doesn't it bother her not to have more pants? I think her limited wardrobe is ridiculous. She can buy more clothes any time she wants.

I know this sounds weird coming from someone who hates

school, but I want to be a teacher. I want to reach out to kids who need help. How cool would it be if my class were a place where students could be themselves? I mean we'd still do work and everything, but there wouldn't be all this stress and nervousness involved. I could connect with kids who feel like outsiders. They'd be able to trust me because I'd know what I'm talking about. Maybe showing them I care will make them feel less alone.

I have a list called Things to Remember When I'm a Teacher. I always keep it in my binder. You never know when inspiration will strike. After observing Mrs. Yuknis's pants trend, I added this to my list:

Have more than four pairs of pants.
Don't wear them on a schedule.

My list is getting long. I started it last year after Carly ripped up my spiral notebook in history. Ms. Herrera totally saw. She didn't even say anything. She just sat at her desk ruffling papers and pretending she wasn't looking. But she totally was. Carly stood right there next to my desk tearing my notebook apart. The pages fluttered to the floor in shreds. I was shocked that Ms. Herrera didn't do anything. I even looked at her like, *Why aren't you doing anything?* Ms. Herrera looked confused. And scared. Like if she made Carly stop, maybe Ms. Herrera would leave school one day and find her tires all slashed. Or her flower garden ripped up. It's so lame. If grownups won't stand up for us, who will?

After Carly finished ripping up my notebook, she stomped on the shreds as she went back to her seat. Then I added this item to my list:

If you see someone being bullied, make it stop.

Why is that so hard for us to do?

◆   ◆   ◆

Mother looks exhausted at dinner. She always looks exhausted. As if just being alive is too strenuous.

There are only a few things mother makes for dinner. Tonight we're having mushy spaghetti with cheap sauce and prepackaged garlic bread.

I bite into a piece of garlic bread. It's still cold in the middle.

My stomach is a tangled ball of knots. You never know what mood mother will be in. This one time last year, she came home really late and woke me up when she slammed the front door. Then she whipped my door open. I could see her glaring at me, the light from the hall illuminating the hate in her eyes. She didn't say anything. She just slammed my door. Then she opened it and slammed it again, harder. I pulled the covers up. I watched my door for a long time, shaking on my thin mattress.

Dinner wouldn't be so stressful if I could eat in front of the TV. I got away with doing that for a while. But then mother started yelling at me to come to the table. If we eat dinner together, she can pretend we're a real family.

"Work is killing me," mother complains. "You wouldn't believe the idiots I have to deal with all day." Then she proceeds to vent about a customer who was trying to return a toaster without a receipt. That kind of thing happens a lot at Retail Rodeo. It's this massive discount store about half an hour away. Mother works in customer service. I can't think of a worse person to work in customer service.

There are plenty of days when mother says less than ten words to me. Sometimes she doesn't answer when I ask her something, like I'm not even there. But tonight she's on a rant of epic proportions. Her rants are almost always about work. Or lack of money. There isn't much else she talks about. The following topics are always avoided: school, people who aren't idiots, female issues, and anything else that normal moms talk about with their daughters.

I can't remember the last time I saw her smile.

Some guy got a promotion at her job. Mother thinks she deserved it more.

"He's the last person who should be general manager," mother says. "That guy doesn't know the first thing about dealing with people."

I twirl more spaghetti around my fork. I'm too hungry to care that it's mushy. Mrs. Feldman is probably serving an amazing meal over at Sherae's house. Thick, juicy cuts of steak. Mashed potatoes made from scratch with extra gravy. Fresh, roasted vegetables. Soft, warm rolls with garlic butter melting on them.

"I can't get a break," mother rants on, looking everywhere but at me. She avoids eye contact. If she saw me, like *really* saw me, she would be forced to face reality. "It's like the whole world's against me. How am I supposed to raise a kid if I can't get paid decently? They have no idea what it's like to be a single mother in this community. None."

There will also be dessert at Sherae's. Mrs. Feldman's chocolate cake is unreal. She makes this vanilla frosting that is so insanely good you can't even believe it. And when she ices the cake, she puts a lot of frosting on. We're talking frosting so thick you get a forkful with every bite.

"They think welfare and food stamps cut it?" Mother laughs bitterly. "What a joke. They should walk in my shoes for a day. They wouldn't even last five minutes."

Moist, delicious chocolate cake. Sweet, rich vanilla frosting.

"I mean, look. I've been there much longer than the idiots who've gotten promoted. He's always trying to keep me down. I should be *his* boss. Then things would start running the way they're supposed to." She takes a sip of soda. "Why can't I ever get a break?"

"Maybe the other customer service reps are nicer to the customers?" I suggest. "And that's why they got promoted?"

Mother snaps her head up. She squints at me in a daze, like she's trying to remember who I am.

"What?" she says.

"Nothing." There's no point in trying to convince her that the conspiracy she's imagining doesn't exist. She's convinced that the whole world is against her. Including me.

Soon this rant will segue into mother complaining how she

has no money. According to mother, it's my fault that we're poor. If she hadn't had me right after high school, then she could have gone to college and had a real career. Instead of making minimum wage at a job she can't stand.

She explained all of this to me when I was thirteen.

"You ruined my life," she told me.

My mother is not a mom. She's just some selfish woman who should have never had a kid.

◆　◆　◆

Things parents are supposed to do for their kids:

- buy needed supplies
- help pay for college
- look at them
- do laundry
- talk to them about their lives
- love them

Things from the above list that my mother does or intends to do:

- none

three

monday, april 11

(49 days left)

My hair is so scary that if you saw it walking down the street, you'd cross to the other side. This humidity is not helping. It's just an excuse for my hair to let its frizz flag fly.

I seriously doubt Jolene DelMonico has to get up way early to deal with hair that refuses to be tamed. She's in my physics class. Every morning her perfect hair is like a smack in the face. Keeping mine shoulder-length helps. I can kind of control it with product, but it's impossible to maintain for more than a few hours. And it's this boring, light brown color that almost exactly matches my eyes.

Unfortunately, my hair isn't the only disgrace I have to deal with this morning. My eyes are puffy. There's no way I can go to school with puffy eyes.

Time for the cold spoon.

I go to the kitchen and grab the spoon I keep in the back of the refrigerator for puffy-eye emergencies. My eyes probably shouldn't get puffy like this. It might be some kind of allergic reaction. But mother never takes me to the doctor, so I guess I'll never know.

In the bathroom, I close my right eye and press the back of the spoon against it. The cold metal soothes my swollen eyelid. My eye waters.

While I'm waiting for the puffiness to calm down, I consider wearing something different from what I decided on. I have on my standard ensemble for the middle of April: jeans and an oversized tee. In the winter, I can get away with wearing bulky sweaters. Or one of the same five long-sleeved shirts I've been wearing since forever. One of them has an oil stain right on the front. I want to throw it out, but I hardly have any clothes.

I'll put on one of my two pairs of Converse before I leave. They're beyond destroyed. But I think all the holes and tears in them look cool. Plus, I write song lyrics and movie quotes all over them. This one time when I was wearing my most destroyed pair, I walked by two popular girls who were sitting against some lockers in the hall. After I passed them, I could hear one of them say, "Did you *see* her shoes?"

I got a little thrill out of that.

By the time I get to school, my hair has puffed up to an alarming amplitude. I don't even have to see myself to know it's atrocious. As much as I hate getting to school early, I appreciate it on days like this. Maybe a miracle will happen where my hair becomes perfectly flat by first period.

You have to wait in the cafeteria if you get to school early. I take my usual seat and try to smooth down my hair. Not a lot of kids get to school this early. It's basically just me and some freshmen in the back. Most mornings I read or do homework. Even when I'm absorbed in studying for a test, part of me is always on alert. Sometimes Julian comes in early. Sometimes he comes over and we talk. Which cannot happen with my hair spazzing out like this. But I can't go anywhere because they won't let you in the halls this early.

There's a new monitor guarding the door. Maybe he'll let me go. I grab my bag and head for the door.

"Going in already?" Julian asks.

I whirl around so fast my bag slams against his leg. "Oh!" I didn't see Julian come in and my hair is outrageous and I just smacked him with my bag. "Sorry!"

"No worries. I thought we were trapped here until the bell."

"We are. I was just trying to make a break for it."

"Sounds scandalous. I'm in."

"Nice." I throw a glance at the monitor. "If you distract him, I can sneak out the far door."

"Distract him how?"

"With a ruckus."

"Right. A ruckus." Julian nods thoughtfully. "Allow me to ponder the nature of said ruckus."

I press down hard on my puffy hair. It refuses to be smoothed. Why does it have to be raining today?

"Got it!" Julian says. "I'll make this sudden commotion like someone just slipped on the floor coming in. That should buy you a few seconds. If you sneak your way over to the door first, you'll have enough time to slip out."

"Sweet."

"But then how will I get out?"

"Hmm." My head is spinning. I can't believe Julian is talking to me despite how repulsive I look. "I'm not sure."

"Let's sit and figure it out."

We sit at the nearest table. And that's when I notice the new silk-screen mural on the wall.

"You finished it!" I say.

"Yeah."

"It's amazing!"

"Thanks."

Julian does these Andy Warhol–type silk screens. I saw some of them in the mixed media elective we had together last semester. Whenever we were working on projects, Julian would come over to my area to see what I was doing. I couldn't believe I was talking to a boy. Who I didn't even know. For the first time ever, I felt like a normal teenager.

That's how I found out he wants to be an architect. He made these gorgeous home designs in class. Houses that were impossibly balanced off cliff sides. Houses that looked like they were floating above water. Houses with trees growing right up through the roof. Julian's designs give you the impression that there are much better ways to live. His philosophy is that your home should be a unique reflection of your personality.

"I can't wait for Sherae to see it," I say. Julian painted a palm-tree mural on the wall. Last week it was just an outline. Then color started to appear. And now it's . . . it's freaking incredible. "She's obsessed with all things California."

"What about you?" Julian asks.

"I don't really think about California. But I definitely can't wait to get out of here."

"I hear you. No, but I meant . . . what are you obsessed with?"

"Oh." *Dir.* "Not much. I mean, you know I like art." I look at his mural again. "That is *so* good."

Julian smiles. It's like he can tell I really mean it.

"You're sweet," he says.

I try smoothing down my hair.

"What kind of art do you like?" he asks.

"You know Alexander Calder?"

"Not personally, but . . ."

I laugh.

He smiles again.

"I like his mobiles," I say. "And I like Brancusi's sculptures. Especially *Bird in Space*."

"I don't know that one."

"Oh, it's gorgeous." I describe the smooth curves of the sculpture. I tell Julian about the time airport customs taxed *Bird in Space* because they thought it was a household item instead of a work of art. Their argument was that the bird didn't have a head, feet, or feathers, so it couldn't be classified as a sculpture.

As I'm telling him all this, Julian leans in closer. He seems even more interested in the story than I was when I read it. Talking to him is always so comfortable. Julian just has this way of making me feel safe.

◆　◆　◆

Ms. Scofield is on one of her TGIM kicks.

"TGIM!" she shouts with way too much enthusiasm for first period. On a Monday. But of course she would only be shouting about TGIM on a Monday. It stands for Thank God It's Monday.

Her concept is this: Why are we all living for Friday? Every single day is an opportunity to improve your life. That's why we should respect all days equally. Monday comes with the added bonus of being the first day of a new week. So not only is it a fresh new day, it's a fresh new week. With tons of potential.

According to Ms. Scofield, that rules.

"Ready to get your Monday on?" she asks us.

We stare at her blankly.

"It's fresh and new," she coaxes.

A prolonged yawn drifts from the back of the class.

At least she's trying to wake us up. She's like the only teacher who understands how hard this is for us. If Ms. Scofield didn't care, physics would be a total drag.

Jolene DelMonico sits in front of me. I'm scandalized by the extreme shine of her hair. If her hair were any shinier, the harsh fluorescent lighting would reflect off it and burn a hole in the Einstein poster. How absurd is it that her hair is pin straight in 100 percent relative humidity? And how absurd is it that I have to sit next to Warner Talbot and pretend he hasn't been harassing me for years? He doesn't just make fun of my lunches. He fired spitballs at me in eighth grade. He kept crank-calling me in ninth grade. And last year he'd do this stupid rap about me every time he saw me in the hall. Now I'm forced to sit next to him like none of that stuff ever happened.

That's what school is. Acting like the things that matter the most don't matter at all.

At least I don't have to work with Warner for activities. Whenever Ms. Scofield tells us to get in pairs or groups, Warner practically hurls his desk in the opposite direction. I work with Ali Walsh in pairs and this girl Darby sometimes joins us for groups. Ali is nice, but she's a loner like me. I don't know much about Darby. She kind of skulks around the periphery.

"Let's turn those brains on triple fab high power!" Ms. Scofield cheers. Then she tings a bell on her desk that's just like the one Retail Rodeo has on its customer service desk. The bell is named Lloyd after a character from one of her favorite movies. Tinging Lloyd is supposed to encourage us to get in gear when she senses that we're fading. Lloyd is also tinged when someone says something fascinating. Or answers an impossible question correctly. Or just to emphasize a point. Lloyd serves many functions.

No one can figure out why Ms. Scofield is always so perky. She doesn't drink coffee. Allegedly. How can her extreme level of perkiness be achieved without caffeine?

"Is everyone ready to start the optics unit?" Ms. Scofield queries. "I know I am. What about you, Gumby?" She picks up the Gumby figure from her desk. Ms. Scofield has a thing for Gumby and Pokey. And this other dude Prickle, who is a yellow dinosaur. She had to explain who they all were at the beginning of the year because only one person recognized Gumby. She puts them in her lessons sometimes. We've also become acquainted with Mr. Bill from old-school *Saturday Night Live.* Whenever we're working on a problem where something falls off a cliff or gets crushed in a ninety-ton hydraulic press, Ms. Scofield will make Mr. Bill the smashed object. Then we'll go, "Oh, nooooo!" Mr. Bill style. It's fun in a retro sort of way.

Ms. Scofield doesn't care that she's corny. She just busted out with all this random stuff on the first day, totally confident about who she is. Even though most of us aren't thrilled about science, we appreciate her effort to try to make it fun. Her confidence is impressive.

School would be way more tolerable if everyone wasn't so afraid to be who they really are. And if everyone else would let them.

◆ ◆ ◆

After school, Sherae drives us to her house. In her new car. How awesome is it that I'm like the only one in our class who doesn't have a car? I don't even know how to drive. Mother's not about to pay for driving lessons. What would be the point, anyway? She would never let me drive her car and there's no way I could buy one. Fortunately, Sherae is incredible about giving me rides.

As soon as Sherae opens the front door, her fuzzy cat comes meowing over. The cat resembles a walking sphere of white fluff. Her name is Nimbus. As in the type of cloud. Sherae's geektastic older brother named her. I like it better around here now that he's away at college. He always gave off this vibe like he was better than me just because he had money. Like I didn't even deserve to be at his house. But if you took away his rich family, we'd be more alike than he would ever admit.

Sherae's mom is unpacking groceries in the kitchen. We go in to help her.

"Hi, Mrs. Feldman," I say.

"Hi, Noelle. How was school?"

"Good." School was actually decent for once. Julian talked to me for a really long time. Warner Talbot left me alone at lunch. My skin miraculously looked okay. And I'm going out with Matt Friday night. Of course I'm dying to tell Sherae all about Matt now that we're official. But I can't. Not that she would tell. I just want to prove to Matt that he can trust me. Anyway, we'll only be a secret for four more days. Then we'll be out in public at the mall for everyone to see. Other kids from school will definitely be there.

We help unpack the groceries. There are eight bags. Eight bags of food for three people. When mother goes grocery shopping, she usually brings home one bag.

I lift out package after package of deli cold cuts. Three kinds of fresh bread. An entire roasted chicken. Tons of fruit and vegetables. Mother prefers to avoid fruit and vegetables. She says they're too expensive. Clearly, Mrs. Feldman does not have the same issue. There's more meat and fish and ice cream and lots of different drinks and chips and pretzels and cookies.

My stomach growls.

"How are you feeling?" Mrs. Feldman asks Sherae.

"Better," Sherae says. She keeps telling me she feels better, too. But I think she's pretending.

Mrs. Feldman doesn't know what happened to Sherae. The next morning, Sherae told her she was sick. Then she stayed home for two days. Mrs. Feldman was here taking care of Sherae because that's what she does. Mr. Feldman doesn't get home until dinnertime. He's a big-shot lawyer.

Sherae puts some fresh-baked chocolate chip cookies (warmed up for us by her mom—how sweet is that?) on a plate while I get drinks. Then we go to her room. I'm accidentally assaulted by my reflection in the big mirror above her dresser.

"Uuuuhhh!" I groan.

"What?"

"Is that what I *look* like?" My hair could not be any frizzier. I press it down. Sherae stands next to me so our eyes meet in the mirror, almost at the same level. She's a little shorter.

"You're so lucky your hair isn't flat," she says. "Mine just hangs there. Yours is pretty."

"If by 'pretty' you mean 'impossible to control,' then yeah."

We've gone over this a million times. I complain about my hair and Sherae complains about hers. But she's just being nice. She has superlight blonde hair that's really fine. It's like sunlight. Plus, she has blue eyes, so she's got that wholesome Girl Next Door thing going on.

I give up trying to make myself look presentable and flop onto Sherae's lounge chair. I could seriously live in this chair. It's a burgundy velvet chaise with a swooping back that's high on one end and then curves down so it's lower on the other end. It is very fancy. When I'm lounging on it, I pretend that I am also very fancy.

The difference between Sherae's room and my room is like the difference between Godiva and Hershey's. Some highlights:

Sherae's Room
- huge
- light and airy
- cute night table
- throw rug in the shape of a poppy flower
- fancy lounge chair
- welcoming

My Room
- microscopic
- dark and dingy
- milk crate masquerading as a night table
- grungy carpeting circa 1964
- calendar where I'm crossing off the days until the end of the year
- embarrassing

My room is The Fortress. I've tried to make it comfortable despite its many flaws. The Fortress is the only place where I can totally relax. Even when I'm with Sherae, I never feel like I can completely be myself.

There's a cootie catcher on the side table next to the lounge chair. Sherae and I love making these. One of us will start making a new cootie catcher. Then we'll pass it back and forth, adding numbers and colors and fortunes until it's done.

The warm cookies smell amazing.

"Here." Sherae brings me three cookies on a napkin. I bite into one. It's slightly crispy on the outside, soft and chewy on the inside. The chocolate chips are almost melted, just the way I like them.

"Ya-*hum*!" I approve. I only have two cookies left. I could eat about a hundred more.

"Want to watch something?" Sherae asks.

"Always."

Nimbus leaps up on the lounge chair. I pet her fluffy fur. She immediately starts purring. Sherae's just sitting on her bed, staring at her wall mural.

"Are you okay?" I ask.

"Hmm?"

I wish I could tell her that she doesn't have to be strong in front of me. But I don't really know what words to use.

"We can just talk, if you want," I say.

"Nope." Sherae gets up and goes over to her entertainment center. In addition to the enormous flatscreen, she has a cabinet filled with a massive supply of fun. "*Freaks and Geeks*?"

"Awesome." *Freaks and Geeks* is one of the best shows ever. Even though it was only on for one season, there's no limit to how many times I can watch those eps. No matter how depressed I am, that show can always make me smile. I even have a poster of James

Franco as Daniel Desario on my wall. And one of Nick Andopolis rocking his disco gear that says YOU'RE TOO TALL TO BE A GOOD DANCER!

Sherae's big wall mural is an Alan Maltz photo of the ocean framed by palm trees, taken during a spectacular sunset. The colors are intense—bold purples and blues, hot pink, and bright red and orange. The photo might have been taken in Florida, but it totally looks like California. Sherae's obsession with California is fierce. She's only applying to colleges in SoCal. She ultimately wants to have a house right on the beach. Which is perfect because she already looks like she's from there.

I can't wait to move far away, but I don't really get why Sherae wants to. I mean, we're both frustrated by the confines of suburban nonliving. But Sherae has the perfect life right where she is. Her parents basically buy her whatever she wants. She even has her own credit card.

Right after I turned sixteen last year, I got a job. Mother told me I had to start saving for college. But I wanted to work. It was understood that she wouldn't be helping me pay for college or anything else.

At the end of last summer, I went to the bank to take out some money for back-to-school clothes. You can't set up your own bank account until you're eighteen, so mother set up the account for me when I got my first paycheck. I couldn't believe I didn't even have to ask her to do that for me. It was the first kind thing she'd ever done.

I followed one of the customer service people to her desk to make the withdrawal because I didn't have a bank card. All of the desks looked the same. No one had any pictures or toys or anything. It seemed like a pretty depressing place to work.

The customer service rep tapped her keyboard.

She said, "There are no funds in that account."

"What?"

"The account has a balance of zero."

"But that's my savings account."

She tapped her keyboard some more.

"When was the last time you made a withdrawal?" she asked.

"I've never made a withdrawal." My heart was pounding. My throat was tight. It was getting hard to breathe. "I've been saving for college."

"Let's see . . . it looks like your mother set up this account for you as a minor, correct?"

I nodded.

"She's been withdrawing funds bi-weekly since your first deposit."

There were times when I'd been furious with mother before. Her neglect was disgusting. But this was a whole new level of furious.

When I got home, mother was drinking a glass of red wine on the couch, staring at nothing.

"Why did you steal my money?" I said.

Mother didn't even bother to look up at me when she said, "It's not your money." She drank more wine.

"Of course it is! It's from my job!"

"Handing people hot pretzels at the mall isn't a real job."

"Um, I get paid? So that's a real job."

"Well, I'm the one paying rent around here. Do you have any idea how expensive that is?"

"What does the rent have to do with saving for college?"

"College?" mother scoffed. "That was rent money."

Blood pounded in my head. I was shaking all over.

"What kind of a freak *are* you?" I yelled. "It's not my responsibility to pay the rent! I'm only sixteen! You're the mother! You're supposed to take care of me!"

"How dare you talk to me that way," mother calmly told the wall.

"I want my money back."

"Too late. It's gone."

"I can't believe you stole my money! You're insane!" I stormed off to The Fortress and slammed my door. Then I opened it and slammed it again even harder, just like mother did that night she scared me so hard I couldn't go back to sleep.

But the slamming wasn't loud enough to wake her up.

◆　◆　◆

The knife is sharp. I'm using a new one tonight.

This is the best way I know how to get lost when I need to escape.

I stick the tip of the X-Acto knife in. I place my index finger on top of the blade and press down hard.

The cardboard pops, then crunches. All I know is that I want this shape to be some sort of squiggle. I'll let the knife take me where it wants to go. The squiggle will be the newest addition to my standing mobile. My neighbors were throwing out this little yellow chair last week. I saw it by their garbage when I was coming home. That night after it got dark, I snuck out and snatched the chair. Now it's the base for all these shapes extending from the chair, suspended by wire.

Calder did these eclectic standing mobiles I adore. I have a thing for simple, modern designs. I'm fascinated by how he combined art and science to create these perfectly balanced objects of beauty. His mobiles have totally inspired mine. I mostly make hanging ones. Since I can't hang my mobiles from the ceiling, I have them hanging all around my room on hooks.

Something about talking to Julian and seeing his finished mural really inspired me. This exciting creative energy has been building up all day. I couldn't wait to get home and work on my mobile. It's cool how Julian's artwork is inspiring my own. I wonder if I'll ever have the courage to tell him about it.

four

wednesday, april 13

(47 days left)

I had a dream that there was this new section of the SATs where you had to fall backward out of a plane. A bungee cord was supposed to pull you back up. Except sometimes the bungee cord didn't work.

I wonder what it means.

◆ ◆ ◆

Here's a secret about me:

I'm a vampire.

Just kidding.

Here's the real secret:

I still ride the bus.

Technically, it's not a secret. If you're like every other junior or senior at my school driving your shiny new car that your mommy and daddy bought you for your seventeenth birthday and you get stuck behind the school bus, you might see me when you finally get impatient enough to pass the bus even though you're not supposed to. You won't find me in the back. That's where the sophomores sit. And the freshmen who make fun of everyone else and throw things at us. No, I sit in the front. Usually next to Jasmine. Who is in sixth grade.

That's right. I ride the bus with sixth graders. We're dropped off at the high school first. Then the bus drives to the middle school, which is even farther away and starts later.

I am the oldest kid riding the bus.

If Sherae didn't have a car, I'd be totally trapped. She would give me rides to school if she didn't live in the opposite direction. But at least we can go wherever we want after school.

My bus stop is right down the street in front of the realty office. The office doesn't open until nine. When the bus drops me off after school, I usually notice one or two people who've come to look at houses. There's a whole new development way back in the woods. Apparently, some people actually want to live in Middle of Nowhere. I don't get it. I mean, yeah, there's lots of space and woods and it's super quiet. So raising kids here might sound like a good idea. But as one of those kids, I could assure them that this town takes boring to a whole other level.

One of the middle school boys comes running down the street just as the bus is pulling up. He's always late. I can't ever be late. If I miss the bus, I have to take the train to school. Which means

I end up missing first period because I have to walk to the train station and wait for the next train and then walk to school from that station. Missing physics is a drag. If you miss one day, you're totally lost.

Everyone piles on the bus. I take my usual seat next to Jasmine. Her bag is way nicer than mine.

♦ ♦ ♦

Carly is waiting for me when I get off the bus.

I don't know why she's so obsessed with bullying me. We used to have the same bus stop. That was the worst. Every morning would be a new adventure in mortification. One time Carly grabbed me by the front of my shirt and pulled her fist back like she was going to punch me. I forget why. She was probably just extra bored that day. A car drove by the bus stop as we were posed like that, Carly threatening to punch me, me frozen like a deer in the headlights. I could see the woman who was driving look at us. She was your typical mom type. She totally saw us. But she drove right by.

"Good morning, Rotten Egg," Carly trills when she sees me. It's her typical greeting.

I brush past Carly, ignoring her. There's no way I could intimidate her. If you put Carly next to a monster truck, the resemblance would be remarkable. She hangs out with the other kids no one wants to mess with. I've heard rumors that she beats up her little brothers. They say that if you ignore a bully, she'll move on to harass someone else. I've been ignoring Carly for three years. She hasn't moved on yet.

"Didn't you hear me?" Carly yells after me. "I said *good morning*!"
I keep on walking.

"Rotten Egg should really learn some manners!" she yells.

People sneak looks at Carly. This one girl makes a nasty face at me. Her friends laugh.

I'm sure all this ignoring Carly will start to work any day now.

The way Carly torments me is bad. But it's nothing compared to the way she torments Ali Walsh. Ali is sweet and quiet and will always let you borrow a pencil. But this is high school. Where it's not about who you are. It's how you look. Ali has really bad skin. And short, frizzy hair. Her wardrobe appears to be visiting from 1993, back when style was really bad. These are the things that define Ali to everyone else. These are the things that convinced Carly she's entitled to pick on Ali anytime she wants.

I saw them in the student parking lot the other day. Sherae and I were going to her car and I noticed Carly way down by the end of the lot. Carly had Ali pinned against the hood of a car, as if Carly were security and Ali needed frisking. I wanted to run over, pull Carly off Ali, and demand that she leave her alone. But I knew if I did that, Carly would torment me even harder. And I can barely get through the day as it is.

So I didn't do anything. I didn't go over. I didn't save Ali.

I hate that I'm so afraid.

◆　◆　◆

When I meet up with Sherae at her locker, she's staring at a note.

"Another one?" I ask.

"It was in my locker."

"What did he say?"

"Same as before. He misses me. He's sorry. Which is hilarious, considering he has no idea what he did." Sherae's eyes fill with tears. "Clueless meathead."

I search my bag for a tissue.

"I'm okay," she insists. "I just don't get how someone could do something like that and not even know how wrong it is."

I wish I had an answer for Sherae. But I've been wondering how people can be so clueless for years.

◆　◆　◆

Ms. Scofield keeps saying how everything is connected. She even has a thing about how science is connected to all other subjects. That's why we had to write optics haikus for homework last week. Before she hands them back, she holds one up.

"This one by Noelle really struck a chord with me," she tells everyone. Then she reads my haiku.

SEEING ≠ BELIEVING

what's in front of you
is not necessarily
the entire story

After class, Simon Bruckner comes up to me. We don't really talk or anything, but he's always been nice to me. I secretly admire Simon. He's kind of an outsider by choice. If he wore ultra-preppy sweaters, pretentious tees, and jeans that cost a fortune but are pretending they don't, he could totally fit in. His parents are supposed to be from one of the wealthiest families around. But Simon doesn't want to be like everyone else. He just wants to be himself. I don't know anyone else who wears trendy ties, fitted vests, and limited edition sneakers. I love his hipster chic style. Today he's wearing a skinny violet knit tie, a polished black dress shirt, black suspenders with violet stripes, distressed dark jeans, and black Converse.

"Hey," Simon says. "I like your haiku."

"Thanks. I like your suspenders."

"I knew you were the type to appreciate style."

That's just Simon being nice. My style is clearly nonexistent.

"Have you read the *Spectrum*?" Simon asks.

The *Spectrum* is the literary magazine. It comes out at the end of the year, right before yearbook. It's a collection of poetry and short stories with some artwork thrown in. I flipped through Sherae's copy last year. Imagine my surprise to discover that I don't have much interest in the thoughts and feelings of privileged snobs.

"Not really," I say.

"I think you should join."

"Me?"

"You."

"Why?"

"You're talented. Teachers always put your writing up. And I need a coeditor. Our last one just quit and I'm already behind."

"Can't someone already on the *Spectrum* be coeditor?"

"In an ideal world, yeah. But none of them wants to work that hard."

"Oh." So Simon just wants me to join because he's desperate?

And he knows I have free time because I have no life? I don't want to say no to Simon right away, though. He's one of the few people who treat me like a human being. "Can I think about it?"

"Oh, for sure. No pressure."

Why do people say "no pressure"? It's like as soon as they say it I feel all this pressure.

"If you could let me know by next week that would be great," Simon adds. "I really need to find a replacement soon."

"Thanks for the offer."

"Thanks for thinking about it." Simon smiles, all confident. Like he could go up to anyone and say anything to them. That must be an awesome feeling.

five

friday, april 15

(45 days left)

I'm going out with Matt Brennan tonight.

No more sneaking off during study hall.

No more hooking up on the DL.

No more keeping our relationship a secret.

After tonight, everyone will know we're together. The last thing anyone wants to do is piss off Matt. And of course Matt will want to protect me. So everyone will stop tormenting me. Including Carly. She rolls with his crowd. Which may be awkward when I start hanging out with his friends, but I'm sure I'll find a way to avoid her.

I cannot wait for my life to get easier.

◆   ◆   ◆

Every time I open my locker, I see all these cool things I taped up. Pictures of me and Sherae. A mini mobile with shapes in primary colors. A postcard of *Bird in Space*. The first cootie catcher Sherae and I made this year.

But when I open my locker this time, all those things are ripped into tiny pieces and scattered over my books.

Awesome.

There's no way I'm going to let my frustration show. Carly is watching from down the hall. I'm sure she's loving this. She can't wait for a reaction.

I'm not going to give her one.

Carefully keeping my expression unchanged, I take what I need out of my locker. Some bits of ripped pictures fall to the floor. I leave them there. I refuse to give her the satisfaction of seeing me pick them up. How did she even get my combination?

Whatever. I'm going out with Matt tonight. I just need to keep focusing on how being his official girlfriend will make all of this go away.

I'm actually smiling when I close my locker.

◆　◆　◆

Sherae and I have this thing where we meet up at her locker before second period. It's tradition.

"Things are looking up," Sherae reports. "No pathetic note from Hector today. And he finally stopped leaving me messages."

"Ooh, that *is* an improvement," I agree.

"Plus! You know that heinous English test I've been stressing? It got postponed!"

"Sweet!"

"Okay. You've been smiling since you got here. What's up?"

"Nothing. Why do you think something's up?"

"Please. Since when are you happy at school?"

"I'm not."

"We're not leaving until you tell me."

I desperately want to tell her about Matt. I *have* to tell her about Matt. Everyone's going to know we're together after tonight anyway. And I've been waiting for this moment for a really long time.

"I have a date," I announce.

"Oh my god!" Sherae gasps. "With who?"

"Matt Brennan."

"You know Matt Brennan?"

"We've been . . ." The bell for second period rings. "It's a really long story. I'll tell you later."

We branch off in separate directions. It's not until I'm at my desk in English that I realize I didn't tell Sherae not to tell anyone about Matt. But of course she won't. That's why she's the only person in the whole world I can trust.

◆　◆　◆

Getting ready for my date with Matt makes it glaringly obvious that I'm in desperate need of a shopping trip with Sherae. Why didn't I ask her to go to the mall this week? I could have gotten a cute top that actually fits. It might be time to rethink this whole baggy look.

This date is already a disaster and I haven't even left my apartment yet.

Sherae drove me home after school and I told her all about Matt. She was not liking our secret status. But I said that not all boyfriends operate on the same schedule. Matt just needed more time. I explained how everything will be out in the open after we're seen together at the mall tonight.

There's no way I was letting Matt pick me up here. He'd probably want to come in. That was not happening. So we're supposed to meet outside Friendly's. Taking the train is my only way to get to the mall. The good news is that the mall is like half a mile from the train station. And there's a back way I can walk between them so no one will know I took the train to get there. Sherae said she'd drive me, but that would be lame.

I write a quick note saying I went to the mall with Sherae. Then I leave before mother can get home and ruin date night with her toxic negative energy. I'm excited just to be going somewhere. Unless I'm hanging out with Sherae after school, I never go anywhere. And even then we pretty much only do stuff before dinner. This is the first time I've been out at night in forever.

When I get to the mall, I walk the long way across the parking lot. This makes it look like I drove here and I'm just coming in from my parking spot. No one takes the train to the mall. No one walks half a mile.

I sit on the bench outside Friendly's and wait. The mall is a world that never changes. No matter what's going on outside, you can always rely on the same overplayed music, bad lighting, and irritated shoppers inside.

Waiting for someone shouldn't be hard. All you have to do is sit there. But it's actually one of the hardest things. When you're sitting by yourself at the mall, you might as well be wearing a flashing neon sign that says LOSER. I try to make it as obvious as possible that I'm waiting for someone. I exaggerate the motions of looking around. I check the time by throwing an exasperated glare at the big clock on the center island. I want anyone who might be watching or passing by my bench to know that alone is just my temporary state. There's a person who wants to be with me. A person who will be here any minute.

Five minutes of waiting turns into ten.

Then twenty.

Half an hour later, Matt still isn't here.

He said Friendly's, right? Did he mean somewhere else?

Matt is thirty-seven minutes late when the worst thing ever happens. A group of kids grabs a window booth at the Olive Garden across from Friendly's.

Of course they're kids from school.

Of course Warner Talbot is one of them.

There has to be a way to hide. The second they look over here, they'll totally see me. Alone on a bench outside Friendly's on a Friday night. Waiting for my secret boyfriend who's almost forty minutes late.

I concentrate on the polished floor. People's shoes walk by. If I don't look up, maybe Warner and those guys won't notice me.

A loud popping noise makes me jump. I turn to see what it was. There's a minor commotion at the candy stand over a big balloon popping. From his booth at the Olive Garden, Warner sees me through the window. His eyes get big. His mouth opens wide. Then he's saying something to his friends and gesturing out the window.

They all turn to look at me. They see me see them.

One of them says something.

They all laugh.

I check the time. Matt is forty-five minutes late.

Maybe something happened. Maybe he was in an accident. He could be in the hospital right now. There's no way for me to know because I don't have a cell phone. I'm not about to call him on the pay phone with everyone watching. Or maybe there was some other emergency. He could come bursting in any second now, saying he's sorry and explaining everything and feeling horrible that I had to wait so long.

Or not.

I wait for over an hour. Shoppers filter on and off of the center island, taking breaks on the benches. They check their devices. They make calls. These two girls have been staring at me. I'm sure they're speculating why I'm still sitting here alone. A disgruntled middle-aged guy has been sitting there for a while. Bags are spread out on the bench next to him. His wife stops by to add three big bags to their collection, then takes off to do even more shopping. The poor guy looks miserable.

Warner is eating and watching me like I'm a movie. One of the girls in the group blows her straw wrapper at him. She says something. The whole table cracks up.

I can't take the humiliation any longer. I get up to leave. Which means that I was officially stood up. And those kids from school saw the whole thing.

◆　◆　◆

As soon as I get home, I check my messages.

There aren't any.

I check my email.

Nothing.

Then I call Matt.

It goes straight to voice mail.

six

monday, april 18

(44 days left)

ꟻ kept thinking Matt would call.

He never called.

That was the longest weekend of my life.

I left a message when I called him Friday night after I got home. It wasn't an angry rant or anything. I just said that I waited a long time for him and that I hoped he was okay and please call me back. When he kept not calling all weekend, I kept wanting to call him again. I wanted to keep trying until he picked up.

But I didn't. It was obvious that he didn't want to talk to me.

I've gone over everything a million times. I can't figure out what I did wrong. What made him change his mind about me?

Am I really that impossible to love?

◆　◆　◆

When I was in ninth grade, the captain of the football team asked me out.

I know. It seems impossible. The most popular guys don't ask out the most unpopular girls.

Unless one of those guys doesn't know who he's talking to.

It was the first day of high school. I was terrified. But for Trevor Burke, it was just the beginning of yet another awesome year of his consistently awesome life. He wouldn't become captain of the football team until the following year, but you could already tell he'd get it. Some people's destiny is understood.

Our algebra class was mainly sophomores. I was ahead one year in math. Trevor was one year behind. That's how he ended up sitting behind me in algebra on the first day of school.

"You're cute," he whispered to me.

Of course I didn't respond. He was just setting me up to believe he actually thought I was cute. Then he would humiliate me in front of the entire class.

I waited for the teasing to continue.

It didn't.

"Can I get your number?" Trevor whispered.

He was serious. I decided to save him some time.

"Ask about me," I whispered back.

"What do you want me to ask?"

"Just ask around. They'll tell you."

"Who?"

"Anyone who knows me. You'll see." I'd given up any hope of being with a boy like Trevor Burke. He existed on a whole other level. The all-American, sun-kissed, handsome football star. The kind of boy parents hope their sons grow up to be.

When Trevor came to class the next day, he didn't look at me. He didn't talk to me ever again.

We belonged to two very different worlds. Even though he sat behind me in algebra.

◆　◆　◆

Sherae is on the warpath.

"He's not getting away with this," she promises at our daily meetup. I was too depressed to call her when I got home Friday night, so I told her about Matt when she called Saturday morning. She was way angrier about it than I was.

"Please don't do anything," I beg. "Let's just wait and see what happens."

"Are you delusional? We already saw what happened. What happened was Matt Brennan being a scumbag."

"But we don't know why he didn't show up yet."

"Because he is a scumbag. That is why."

"Maybe he—"

"No."

"He could have—"

"No."

"But—"

"He needs to apologize. I find it highly suspect that he hasn't yet."

"Just . . . I'll take care of it."

"Are you sure? Because I'm ready to rumble."

"Yeah, Ponyboy. I picked up on that."

◆ ◆ ◆

Spontaneous eye contact with Julian Porter has only happened a few times at lunch. Usually, I'll just sneak glances at him. Sometimes I can feel him looking at me. Or I'll see him looking at me out of the corner of my eye, but I'll pretend that I don't.

Attempting eye contact at lunch always involves a huge degree of risk. If I'm trying to look at Julian without looking like I'm actually looking and I accidentally look at someone else, there could be a problem. They could take it as an invitation to launch a verbal attack.

Tommy's sitting alone again at his usual table. Apparently, having money isn't always enough to avoid persecution. It's amazing how two rejects like us can force everyone else to deal with having two less tables available. I guess we have some power in a warped way.

When I got to the cafeteria, I tried to anticipate where Warner and those guys would sit. Then I picked a table far from there. Most kids sit at the same table every day. But with Warner, it's like this incessant game of musical tables we're playing where he's the only one having fun.

Of course Warner sits at the table behind mine. His friends immediately swoop in after him.

"What's for lunch?" Warner asks from behind me. I don't turn around. I know his question is meant for me. I'm reading. Which at lunch mostly consists of pretending to read. But I find that when I read or listen to music in here, people pretty much leave me alone.

I keep Pretend Reading.

"Lettuce sandwich again?" Warner inquires. "Ooh, or maybe you got the mayonnaise and mustard one this time! Aren't those the *best*?"

"Maybe her mom wiped her butt and put that in a sandwich," his friend says.

Warner's whole table cracks up. I hear the slap of a high five.

My face burns. I stay as still as possible in Pretend Reading mode. If I make any kind of move like switching seats, they'll know they're getting to me. And that will just make it worse.

My lunch bag of sorry kitchen scraps remains unopened on the table. I can't deal with it today. I'm just relieved that Julian's sitting like five tables away. If he heard what Warner and his friend said to me, I would die.

I peek at Julian. He isn't looking.

There's a group of girls at the table in front of mine. They look so happy, talking and laughing like school's the most comfortable place in the world. I know their names. I know the clubs they belong to and the instruments they play and the teams they're on. But I can never really know them. Not anymore.

I tried to sit with them on the first day of school. They said all the seats were taken. I used to be really good friends with some of them. They'd come over to my house to play and I'd go over theirs. That was back in elementary school before mother started to change. Back when she was almost like a real mom.

Before we moved to our apartment, mother and I lived with Lewis in a big house like everyone else. Mother met Lewis when

I was two. He was a professor at the college near the bar and grill where she worked. He went there for lunch and always sat in mother's section. His wife had divorced him and moved to France a few years before. His kids were in college. He had the whole house to himself.

Living with Lewis was nice. I had most of the same things other kids had. There was lots of room. There was always enough to eat. And I could have friends over without feeling like I had to hide anything. I even had a huge birthday party in third grade. My entire class came. Back then, it felt like I fit in. It felt like I had a place to belong.

Then Lewis got cancer.

He died when I was eleven. Lewis and mother weren't married, so we had to move out. He left the house to his oldest son. Most of his savings went to his other kids and relatives. Lewis left mother some money, but he didn't have much to leave and she used it up quickly. She didn't want to move to another town. That's when she found our apartment. That's when people she thought were her friends started fading away. And that's when I started lying.

Lying isn't something I ever wanted to do. I lied because I had to. When mother stopped taking care of me, I made up this story about how she was in the hospital. Which somehow evolved into this whole big thing about how she might die. I was only trying to justify my humiliating clothes and lunches. The plan was to tell everyone she got better after a few weeks. But my friends found out I lied. One of them saw mother at the post office and told everyone. Sherae was the only one who didn't hate me. People started calling me a liar. Warner started making fun of my lunches. Carly started bullying me. And they never stopped.

The thing is, I don't entirely regret that I lied. I'd rather have the whole school hate me than everyone know my truth.

The girls at the next table are laughing again. I refuse to open my flat lunch bag. Pretending I'm looking at the clock, I peek at Julian.

He's looking right at me.

I look back at him.

He doesn't look away.

He smiles at me.

I smile back.

And then a gob of something smacks into the back of my head.

The girls at the next table stare. Warner's table is roaring with laughter.

No one comes over to help me.

More kids turn to look. It gets eerily quiet.

I do not want to know what's in my hair.

I have to know what's in my hair.

I reach back and tentatively touch the gob. It's mashed potatoes.

Warner finds this to be hilarious.

But that's not even the worst part. The worst part is that Julian saw the whole thing. He was looking right at me when it happened.

Julian Porter just saw me get smacked in the head with a gob of mashed potatoes.

There's only one option.

I stand up, grab my things, and head for the door. Some mashed potatoes slide down my hair and hit the floor with a splat. Kids are giving me wide eyes and covering their smirks and gawking as I pass them.

I slam against the door to push it open. The monitor is yelling at me that I can't leave. I want to yell back that he should do his job. Where was he when the mashed potatoes were flying?

But I don't yell. I don't say anything. I just leave. And I'm never going back.

seven

tuesday, april 19

(43 days left)

Study hall is a lot less interesting when you're not making out with a hot boy. I thought about cutting. But where would I go?

I'm about to take out my physics worksheet when something outside catches my eye. These windows overlook the student parking lot. Carly and Audrey are messing around out there like they don't even care that anyone could see. When I sneak out to hook up with Matt, I always use the side door by the gym. There aren't any windows down there. And our place is so desolate that no one's ever caught us. But Carly and Audrey are practically daring someone to catch them. Carly is sitting on Audrey's hood. Audrey is telling a story with lots of animated hand motions.

It's so weird that Audrey hangs out with Carly now. I've watched her go from a Pretty Perfect Popular girl to getting tangled up in this bad-girl phase. What would make a person trade in that life for this one?

◆　◆　◆

I have a plan. It's temporary, but it should let me avoid the cafeteria for the rest of the week. Instead of shuffling along with everyone going to lunch, I'm pretending that I have to get something from my locker. I keep pretending until the bell rings.

When the halls are almost empty, I take out my flat lunch bag. This is the tricky part. There's usually a monitor standing just inside the cafeteria door trying to herd in loiterers. If he catches me darting for the stairway near the door, he'll yell at me to come back. The dude knows who has lunch when.

I head toward the cafeteria. The monitor's stationed at his spot by the door. There's a loud banging noise from inside. Kids start yelling. He goes to investigate.

Now's my chance.

I lunge for the stairway and fly downstairs. The girls' room is near this end of the hall. Teachers down here have already started their next class. So the chances of getting caught in the hall are slim.

I slowly press the bathroom door open. I don't hear anyone inside. I go in. Still no one. I quickly look under the stalls. They're empty. I go inside the last stall, lock the door, and wait.

No one comes in.

Sitting on the toilet with my feet up, I uncrinkle my lunch bag as quietly as possible. If someone comes in, I'll stop uncrinkling until they leave. I unpack my "lunch." There wasn't any bread to make a sandwich, so I just have a store-brand toaster pastry and some raisins. I gobble everything down.

My stomach growls for more.

I keep replaying yesterday's cafeteria scene. How Julian was looking right at me when I snuck a look at him. How he didn't look away. How he smiled at me.

How that gob of mashed potatoes splattered against my head.

I'll never be able to face Julian again.

◆　◆　◆

There's a note in my locker before gym.

> Noelle,
>   Sorry about what happened. Meet me at our place tomorrow.
>   Please?
>
>   —Matt

If he's so sorry, why didn't he call me back? Or write why he didn't show up in his note? Plus, he's obviously been avoiding me in the halls.

I shouldn't meet up with him. But of course I will. I want to hear what he has to say. And I'm not about to randomly confront him or anything.

Matt can't just throw away our entire relationship. You don't feel one way about somebody and then feel a totally different way two seconds later. There has to be a good reason why he didn't show up.

If Matt doesn't want me, no one will.

◆　◆　◆

When the last bell rings, I almost trip over myself racing to my locker. I fling it open and start shoving stuff in my bag. Being alone before mother gets home is the only time I can breathe. I'm already anticipating my stress level dropping when I get to The Fortress, put on my yoga pants, and start reading on my bed.

"Hey," Julian says.

The textbook I was about to put in my bag drops to the floor. It somehow manages to fling itself open in midair, hitting the floor with a sloppy smack.

"Hey," I say.

He bends down to pick up my book.

How can my heart be pounding this hard without busting an artery?

"Sorry about yesterday." Julian hands me my book. The corners of some pages are bent. When I take it from him, I swear I can feel electricity zing from his side of the book to mine. Miraculously, the book does not burst into flames.

"What do you mean?" I ask.

"About what happened at lunch. Those guys are morons."

I can feel my face getting red. I stick my head in my locker, pretending to look for more things I need to take home. This is the part where Julian says he has to go and then he leaves and never talks to me again. Why would he want to be seen associating with such a freak?

But that's not what happens. Julian's still here.

"I looked for you at lunch today," he says.

"Oh. I'm doing this thing fifth period now, so I won't be in that lunch anymore."

"What thing?"

"Just this thing for lit mag." I have no idea where that came from. I don't even want to join lit mag.

"That's cool. I didn't know you were on lit mag."

"I just joined." Why am I such a lying liar? Do I really think Julian won't find out I'm not on lit mag?

"Do you like it?"

"It's . . ." I close my locker. "Yeah, it's fun. I'm—" I almost say *I'm going to miss my bus.* Then I catch myself. "I have to go."

I cannot leave fast enough.

◆　◆　◆

In an alternate universe, Julian Porter and I would be together. I'd have a normal home life with parents who love me. No one would have any reason to torture me at school. I'd fit right into Julian's world.

But we're in this universe.

I'm sure he doesn't even like me. But let's say he did. There's no way he could ever come over. He'd see my corroded apartment. He'd see how there's never anything to eat. He'd see how my closet is practically empty. And what a lunatic my mother is.

Assuming he didn't immediately run away after witnessing my pathetic existence, then what? We'd start going out. We'd get closer. And eventually our clothes would start coming off. I am the proud owner of exactly two bras that fit. Sexy much? Before I go to bed, I hand wash the bra I wore that day and hang it up to dry. The other one is usually dry in time to wear the next morning. If not, I finish drying it with my blow-dryer. I'd use my babysitting money to buy more, but bras are expensive. It's all about saving enough to get out of here. One day when I can afford nice things, I'm going to have one whole drawer with fancy bras and another whole drawer with matching panties. They'll all have cute colors and fun patterns. My tattered, old underwear will be a distant memory.

Anyway. I'm sure Matt is going to explain himself tomorrow and everything will go back to our version of normal. Which is the most I can hope for right now.

eight

wednesday, april 20

(42 days left)

"So where were you?" I ask Matt. He was waiting for me when I got to our place.

"It was stupid of me not to show," he says. "I'm sorry."

"Where were you?"

"At home."

"You stayed *home*?"

"I wanted to see you, but it was like . . . suddenly there was all this pressure to make things official."

"But we've been together for over a month."

"It doesn't work that way for guys. We don't go, 'Oh look, this much time has passed, now things need to get serious.'"

"Then why'd you ask me out if you didn't want to go out with me?"

"I *do* want to go out with you. I just don't think I'm ready to make it public yet." Matt comes over and puts his arms around me. I love it when he holds me. It makes me feel wanted.

"Why not?" My voice is muffled by his motorcycle jacket.

"My last girlfriend burned me. She kinda went psycho. Totally humiliated me in front of my friends."

"I wouldn't do that to you."

"I know. I'm just not ready to announce that I have a new girlfriend." He rubs my back in slow circles. "Can you give me a little more time?"

This is the first time Matt has called me his girlfriend. Which makes it hard for me to stay mad at him. I'm sure it won't be much longer until he's ready to tell everyone about us. And I mean, what, like I've never done anything stupid? We all do things we regret. My past is packed with things I wish I could take back. And there are lots of things I'm afraid of. Fear is understandable. So I can forgive Matt for being scared.

"Okay," I tell him.

We spend the rest of third period making up.

◆　◆　◆

It's official.

I'm on lit mag.

It's not like I'm joining yearbook. Yearbook is such a lie. It only has pictures of the popular kids. One time part of my arm snuck into a yearbook picture. I wrote *My arm!* with an arrow indicating the correct arm. That's the closest I've ever come to being included in the yearbook. Other than my dorky school pictures, which are consistently repulsive.

I didn't join lit mag just because I told Julian I was already on it. Simon said I could use the lit mag office fifth period when he's in there. Which gives me a valid excuse to get out of lunch. The faculty advisor, Mr. Gilford, doesn't care if you eat in there because that's when most of the other kids have lunch. So not only am I excused from the cafeteria for the rest of the year, but I get to hang out with someone really cool. Maybe we'll even become friends.

This. Is awesome.

"As coeditor, you get your own desk," Simon tells me. "It comes complete with wheely chair." Simon demonstrates that the chair indeed rolls by pushing it back and forth. Then he shows me how everything else in the lit mag office works and explains what I'm supposed to do. "Do you know how to use the editing program in Word?"

"I don't think so."

"No worries, it's really simple. I'll show you."

Simon is rocking his typical metrosexual hipster look. Today he has a worn maroon tee that says HOLLA BACK in yellow seventies bubble letters, a black vest, dark skinny jeans, and black combat boots. I love how he never seems to care what anyone thinks. The wild thing is, it makes them leave him alone. Trying to ignore a bully when you're bothered by what they're doing is completely different from not caring. They can tell you're trying really hard to ignore them when you care. They know they're getting to you, which makes them want to harass you even more.

But Simon's not playing. He really is that confident. Sometimes people say stuff about his ties or his hair. He has tousled, wavy brown hair and he's not afraid to use the product. If anyone snarks at Simon, he just snarks right back full force. The boy is impressive. Like when we were going to lit mag, Simon was singing some Bee Gees song.

In the middle of the hall.

In a falsetto voice.

Loudly.

A bunch of Pretty Perfect Popular girls glared at Simon like he was an escaped mental patient. Which of course made Simon sing even louder. He sang right at the girls, flashing them the peace sign.

Simon Bruckner is my hero.

◆ ◆ ◆

Sherae comes running up to my locker.

"Did your hear?" she says.

"About what?"

She pauses for dramatic effect. "Julian Porter and Warner Talbot got into a scuffle."

"What? Where?"

"In gym. Apparently, they had some kind of confrontation playing basketball. I heard that Julian knocked Warner down. And when Warner tried to get up, Julian pushed him down again."

That is so unlike Julian. He never gets in trouble.

"Julian was totally defending your honor," Sherae says.

"He was not."

"He obviously *was*! Why else would he be pushing Warner around?"

Sherae is ridiculous for thinking Julian was defending me. But the possibility that it might be true makes me happy.

◆ ◆ ◆

When I get up from my chair after precalc, my heart slams against my chest in a surge of panic.

I cannot believe this happened again.

No one else seems to be noticing. Everyone's shoving papers in their notebooks and rushing to go home. I linger at my desk, flipping through my day planner. I wait until everyone's gone. Then I look back down at my chair.

There's blood.

My blood.

This hasn't happened since ninth grade. That was before Sherae had a car and she started taking me to the mall so I could get what I needed. Back then, I didn't have anyone to help me get the things mother should have been getting.

Good thing I'm wearing dark jeans. I've learned to get creative with toilet paper, but it's not a reliable method. There's no way I'm going to the nurse. I'd feel even more embarrassed begging her for tampons.

I drop my pencil on the floor and slowly bend over to pick it up, just in case anyone comes in. I check my jeans. You can't really see anything from the back. I should be able to get to my locker without any drama. There's an old cardigan I always keep in there for emergencies. I'll wrap it around my waist. Luckily, Sherae's not waiting for me today. I don't want her to see me like this. I'll have to take the late bus.

But first, I have to get this blood off the chair.

I rummage through my bag until I find a copy of the school newspaper. I put that on my chair, covering up the stain. Then I put my bag on top of the newspaper and go to my locker. Kids are yelling and slamming lockers and leaving. No one notices me.

Please don't let Carly be here.

I make it to my locker and tie the cardigan around my waist. Then I get a few wet paper towels from the bathroom. I scrub my chair. The paper towels work. I quickly wipe the seat clean and dry it. You can't even tell what happened.

Not like last time.

When this happened two years ago, it was the middle of the day. I got up, saw the blood, and there was nothing I could do about it. The next class was already coming in. There wasn't any time to clean my chair. I was horrified that I had to leave it stained, but I didn't have a choice.

I ran out before anyone saw.

In the hall, I could hear the boy who sat there after me complaining. He yelled how there was no way he was sitting there and that was disgusting and who sat there before him?

Of course Ms. Morrison knew it was me. I had no idea how I'd ever be able to face her again. And she had no idea I was sort of friends with Ali Walsh, who was in her next class with Yelling Boy. So Ms. Morrison assumed I wouldn't find out what happened next.

She took out a box of latex gloves, pulled a pair on, and got out some Windex and a roll of paper towels. Then she cleaned the chair while everyone freaked out. Freshmen are the worst. Ali told me that everyone was making retching noises and period jokes and Caitlin Holt actually screamed. As if the blood were going to spurt off the chair and destroy her couture. Ali didn't want to tell me any of this, but I made her. I needed to know how bad it was.

After Ms. Morrison cleaned the chair, she told Yelling Boy to sit down.

He would not.

"There's no way I'm sitting on that," he repeated. "It's contaminated."

"You just saw me clean it," Ms. Morrison said.

"Windex doesn't cut it, miss."

Ms. Morrison ripped some fresh paper towels off the roll. She put them on the chair.

"Germs can't travel through a paper boundary," she explained. "I'll make sure the janitors clean the chair later."

That sounded like a crock, but it worked. Yelling Boy sat down and shut up. Which should have been the end of it.

But it wasn't. He showed up early the next day to see who sat there before him.

It didn't take long for the whole school to hear that I'm a chair contaminator.

❖ ❖ ❖

Item on Things to Remember When I'm a Teacher list:

If a student needs help, help them.

Something tells me I won't forget this one.

❖ ❖ ❖

The phone rings as I'm studying for a Spanish test. I'm assuming it's a bill collector. So I'm not exactly jumping out of my chair to get the phone. But if I don't get it, mother will barge in and make me. She always forces me to answer and tell bill collectors she's not here. Avoiding unnecessary mother drama is always the best tactic.

I pick up the phone in the kitchen.

"Hello?"

"Hi, is Noelle there?"

"This is Noelle."

"Hey, it's Julian."

I'm shocked into silence. Julian never calls me. *Ever.*

"Julian Porter?" he says. "From school?"

"Yeah, no, I . . . hey."

"Are you studying for our Spanish test?"

"Ugh." I run into the living room to make sure mother's not in there. "That preterite conditional is killing me." She must be in her room. But her door is halfway open. She could be listening to my entire conversation. "What about you?" I run back to the kitchen, trying to keep my breathing steady.

"Haven't even started."

"Good luck with that."

"Thanks."

I hunker down against the farthest cabinet. Mother shouldn't be able to hear me this way. I've caught her spying before.

"So . . ." Julian says. "Do you ever go into the city?"

"Not as much as I want to."

"It's awesome there."

"Like a whole other world."

"Do you want to go with me sometime?"

Wait. Is Julian Porter asking me out?

"It doesn't have to be like a . . . date," Julian says. "Or whatever. We could just go have some fun."

"I like fun."

I like fun? Seriously?

"Cool, so—"

"But I can't go."

"Oh."

I desperately want to say yes. But even if we just went as friends, it wouldn't be right. I could never do that to Matt. I'd hate it if Matt hung out with some girl he liked.

"It's just . . . it's complicated," I say.

"Bummer. Well, I guess I'll just have to have fun without you."

I can't believe this is really happening. I can't believe Julian doesn't know he's too good for me. Maybe he doesn't see it now. But eventually, he will. And he'll realize he's better off without me.

nine

thursday, april 21

(41 days left)

M*s*. Scofield *is* extra perky today.

"Inertia!" she cheers. "Bet you didn't know that our optics unit relates to Newton's Laws. But it does. Everything is connected. So. Who remembers Newton's First Law?"

We all avert our eyes to prevent getting called on.

"Like I'm really going to believe you guys forgot Newton's Laws? You're smarter than that."

I hear someone flipping through their notes in the back. Jolene DelMonico raises her hand.

"Yay!" Ms. Scofield says. "A sign of life! What can you tell us?"

"An object in motion remains in motion and an object at rest remains at rest unless acted upon by an outside force."

"Exactly. So things keep doing what they're doing unless something comes along to change that. That's inertia."

She grabs the Gumby and Pokey figures that are always smiling at us from her desk. She's had them since she was in high school. One time she said how she wished she had more stuff from high school to show us and how she regrets not keeping her journals. I wonder why she got rid of all those things.

"Gumby and Pokey will now demonstrate inertia." Ms. Scofield places them on the demo table.

Then she just watches them. We watch her watch them.

"What's happening?" she asks.

"Nothing," Warner calls out.

He's sharp, that one.

"Can you be more specific?"

"They're just sitting there."

"Why?"

"Because nothing's making them move."

"Aha!" Ms. Scofield yells. Ali's book falls off her desk with a loud smack. "So something has to happen to change their inaction. They'll keep being still like this until something comes along to change their static state. For Gumby and Pokey, inertia means that they'll stay exactly like this unless an outside force makes them move in some way."

I know all about inertia. This town is squishing me down like a bug it really wants to kill, but is having too much fun torturing.

"But then!" Ms. Scofield smacks Gumby. Gumby goes flying toward the door. "An outside force puts Gumby into motion." Gumby skitters across the floor and stops. "And now he's at rest again. What made Gumby stop moving?"

"Friction," a few people offer.

"Nice. You guys sound tired. Feeling tired today?" Ms. Scofield picks up Pokey. She puts him on her head.

"Awesome," Simon declares. He snaps a picture of Ms. Scofield with his phone.

"That phone's not on, is it?" she asks him.

"Of course not. It's on airplane mode."

"Doesn't 'on airplane mode' mean it's on?"

"It's not *on* on," Simon clarifies. "Just minimally on."

I love how Ms. Scofield is having a regular conversation like a rubber pony isn't standing on her head. She's never afraid to look like a nerd. On the first day, she told us that she's the nerdiest person in the room. And that no one should even try to have a dork-off with her because they would drastically lose that battle. Her corny, zany teaching style works. I'm pretty sure we'll always remember inertia after watching Gumby go zinging across the room.

Inertia and I go way back. An object remains at rest unless acted upon by an outside force. Story of my life.

I wonder what my outside force will be.

◆　◆　◆

I tried calling Sherae last night right after I got off the phone with Julian, but her phone was off. She's been turning it off a lot lately. At first I thought it was to avoid Hector's calls, but she said he stopped calling her so I don't know. She wasn't online, either. I left a message saying I had something major to discuss at our daily meetup.

Sherae is violently ripping up a piece of paper at her locker.

"Another note?" I ask.

"The dumbass strikes again. So what's going on?"

"Oh, nothing." There's some white Nimbus fur on the sleeve of her black cardigan. I brush it off. "Just that Julian asked me out."

"He asked you *out*?!"

I nod.

"When?"

"He called me last night."

"Why didn't you tell me?"

"I tried. Your phone was off and you weren't online."

"Dude. He is so in love with you."

"Hardly."

"What did you say?"

"What do you think?"

"That you realize Matt is a skeeze and of course you'll go out with Julian?"

"First off, Matt is not a skeeze. It just takes him a while to open up to people. And I couldn't go out with Julian even if I wasn't with Matt."

"Why not?"

I give Sherae a look like, *Isn't it obvious?*

"Why *not*?" she demands.

"I'm not . . . enough for him."

"How can you think that? He totally likes you. I told you that fight with Warner was about you."

"Whatever. It doesn't matter. I'm with Matt."

"But you have a choice. You don't have to be with Matt. You could be with Julian."

"Maybe I want to be with Matt. Maybe that's why I'm with him."

"Or maybe you're afraid to have something real with a boy who clearly adores you."

"Matt adores me."

"Really? Because last time I checked, he stood you up. Oh, and he refuses to be seen with you in public."

Why does Sherae have to be so nasty about this? Just because Matt isn't acting the way she wants him to doesn't make him unworthy. I know he cares about me. He just needs more time, is all.

Not that I'm about to explain all this to Sherae again. It's better just to drop it. I cannot get in a fight with her about this. Or about anything. She's the only person I can completely count on to be there for me.

◆　◆　◆

Hooking up with Matt is hotter than ever. I wish we could stay out here at our place forever. I love how it's like we're hidden from the rest of the world. I love how nice it is out. And I love how Matt is making me feel. I can't remember the last time I felt this good.

Matt kisses me with fierce intensity. I kiss him back even harder.

We *so* need to get a room.

It's hard to believe that having sex with an actual boy is a possibility for me. My relationship with Matt is nothing like what I wish I had with Julian. It's not like Matt's about to come over after school for fresh-baked cookies. We'd probably just end up doing it in the back of his car or something. Matt totally wants to do it. So do I. I think. I mean, my hormones definitely want to. But something is holding me back. We haven't even been together that long. I just don't want to rush into anything before I absolutely know for sure that I'm ready.

Not that deciding to wait makes me want to do it any less.

◆   ◆   ◆

I'm really nervous about seeing Julian in class. What do you say to the boy you rejected last night? Do you smile at him to see if he's mad? Do you ignore him so he won't be embarrassed? Do you pretend like nothing happened?

Julian's already at his desk when I get to Spanish. He doesn't look at me. When class ends, he's out the door before I even have my stuff together.

I take my time walking to lit mag. It's not like I'll get in trouble for being late. If I wanted to, I could even go the long way down the hall where Julian's locker is. Not that I'd see him. The way he raced out of class, he's probably at lunch already.

I go down his hall anyway.

And there he is.

Two of Julian's friends are at his locker. I've had classes with them, but we've never talked or anything. Still, you can tell they're not like all the standard obnoxious boys who go here. They might even like me if Julian and I were together. It could be this whole new world of friends.

Julian's laughing at something one of his friends said. His glasses frames are catching the light in that way that makes them glint electric blue. Right before he slams his locker, I see his messenger bag inside with the orange star on it. Everything about Julian Porter shines.

◆   ◆   ◆

Sherae declared the need for some serious mall time after school. I'm looking forward to zoning out in that groggy daze induced by artificial foliage and the comforting aroma of Auntie Anne's pretzels. The mall we go to is forty minutes away. It's massive. The smaller mall closer to town is where Matt and I were supposed to go. Most kids from school go there. Which is why we come here.

Even though the massive mall is in another suburb, it feels like a city to me. The town has a more urban feel. It has actual things to do. There's a zing of excitement in the air, like you know things are happening all around you even if you don't know what they are.

Sherae turns onto the road that leads to the highway that leads to the suburban city and, eventually, the real city. This is The Road. The Road leads to Not Here. Which is the best place ever. It's the road to freedom. It's the road to a better life, to a place where dreams have a chance to become reality.

The first thing we do at the mall is get ice-cream cones. Sherae gets strawberry dipped in chocolate. I get vanilla with rainbow sprinkles. Rainbow sprinkles make me happy.

I'm relieved we're here. I knew I should have gotten another box of tampons the last time we were here, but I couldn't sneak away from Sherae long enough. I'd be mortified if she knew that mother didn't get them for me. There's no way I could admit how bad things are.

It's hard to be surrounded by everything shiny and new and not buy lots of things for myself. There's so much I want. But I've been very strategic about saving ever since mother stole my money. When I get paid for babysitting, I divide the cash and hide it around my room so mother can't find it. She doesn't know that I babysit almost every weekend, so it's not like she's wondering where all my money is. I told her that I babysit like once a month and that I spend the money on school supplies.

We sit by the fountain to eat our ice-cream cones.

"So . . . what did Hector's note say?" I ask.

"Just that I can't keep ignoring him forever and why won't I talk to him."

"Why is he acting like he didn't do anything?"

"He said he doesn't even know what he did. Just that I expected him to apologize for something."

"How can he not know?"

Sherae licks her ice cream.

I feel horrible that Sherae has to go through this. If I could switch places with her to take away her pain, I would. She doesn't deserve any of this.

I say, "But do you—"

"I'm fine." Sherae gets up and throws the rest of her ice cream out. She didn't even eat the cone. Which I know is her favorite part.

Hector used to take Sherae out for ice cream all the time. He only likes ice cream in the summer, but he'd take her anyway. It was obvious that Hector adored Sherae. Every time I saw them together, he was either holding her hand or he had his arm around her. Or he was kissing her and I was trying not to look. He gave her special gifts that boys wouldn't normally think of, like the palm tree snow globe she loves. Or loved. She either put it away somewhere or got rid of it after they broke up. They had a pretty good relationship. But Sherae wasn't ready for what Hector wanted. And once you cross that line, there's no going back.

Maybe Sherae is hiding from me just like I'm hiding from her. Maybe she thinks that if she keeps saying she's okay, her emotions will believe her. Like how if you smile enough times you can trick your brain into thinking you're happy.

Next up is the drugstore. Sherae never needs anything here. She gets a lollipop with a long stem and a cute pink watermelon bobbing on top. We're not splitting up, so I try to play off the whole getting tampons thing like mother just forgot to buy more. I hope I sound convincing without trying too hard.

"Where to next?" Sherae says.

"What about the pet store?" I always stop by the pet store when I'm here. They have such tiny, adorable puppies in the window. I love watching them, but I can only watch for a few minutes. They make me want to cry after that. If I had a pet, I would be constantly worrying that something horrible was about to happen to him. I wouldn't be able to just enjoy the time we had together like a normal person. I'd be too worried about my inevitable breakdown after he was gone.

On our way to the pet store, we pass a group of boys around

our age. They all look at Sherae. None of them looks at me. Sherae pretends not to notice them looking. She doesn't even make eye contact with boys anymore.

I wish they would look at me. But why would they? I'm a walking freak show of oversized tee and destroyed sneakers and frizzy hair.

"Let's go to Forever 21," I say.

"What about the puppies?"

"Later." I want to see if they have any new tees I can afford. Forever 21 is good about prices. I have fifteen dollars left from the stash I allowed myself to take with me today. There has to be a cute top in there for fifteen dollars. One that actually fits for a change. I'm tired of never being noticed.

◆ ◆ ◆

"Can you let me out here?" I ask Sherae as she's driving me home. There's a random weekday garage sale a few blocks from my place that I must explore.

Sherae knows the drill. I scavenge at garage sales for things to make my room look nicer. I found a purple scarf to drape over my ripped lampshade. I painted an old vase and put some fake daisies in it that my neighbor was throwing out. An old photo box holds my jewelry.

There's a bin of random fabric scraps. I find a pretty piece of turquoise silk. It looks like it will be the perfect size.

"How much is this?" I ask an old man with an enormous gut sitting at a card table.

"Two dollars."

When I get home, I clear my milk crate masquerading as a night table. I dust everything off. I shake out the turquoise silk and drape it with a flourish over the piece of wood that sits on the crate. It goes really well with the purple scarf on my lamp. Then I carefully arrange everything on top. It almost looks like I have a real night table now.

Trying to make things look nice takes a lot of effort. But I will never stop trying.

ten

monday, april 25

(39 days left)

Good thing every day starts with announcements in homeroom. I'd hate to miss out on any pep rallies.

The first announcement notifies us of the following vital information:

"The Bulldogs are away tonight at Lakeview. Game starts at six. Let's all go out and show our support!"

Apparently, announcements are now in code. Because I have no idea who the Bulldogs are or what they're playing.

Then:

"Yearbook order forms *must* be submitted to the main office by the end of the day. Don't miss out on the memories!"

Right. I wouldn't want to forget any of those.

◆   ◆   ◆

Simon comes into physics all adult with his polished style and car keys and coffee cup. The car keys clank down on his desk. He takes the lid off his cup and blows on his coffee. I don't think Simon sees school the same way we do. It's more like he's arrived at work, sipping his expensive coffee drink and looking out the window like it's just another day at the office.

Simon glances around the room at the other kids coming in as if he's about to conduct a business meeting. Then he comes over to me.

"Hey, Noelle," he says. "You look like you're in the mood for some extra work."

"How could you tell?"

"I'm intuitive like that. We just got a new stack of submissions that need to be edited by next Monday. Could you work fifth period every day this week?"

Is he serious? If I could, I'd keep going to lit mag fifth period every day for the rest of the year.

"Yeah," I say.

"Sweet. So I'll see you later?"

I nod. Simon Bruckner has totally saved me from cafeteria hell. Even with all the work I'm doing for lit mag, I still majorly owe him.

◆ ◆ ◆

I made out with Matt too long and now I'm late for Spanish. I knew I should have left fifteen minutes earlier, but it was impossible. My lips just did not want to leave his lips.

Instead of going straight to Spanish after study hall, I had to go see Mr. Gilford. He needed to confirm that I don't have a class fifth period. He gave me a special pass that says I'm allowed to be in the lit mag office fifth period and after school. Then he gave me a late pass for Spanish. Which is a small price to pay for being crazy with lust.

Normally, I hate making entrances. Being late is a whole different thing when you're me. When Pretty Perfect Popular girls come into class late, they're fine with everyone looking at them. Why wouldn't they be? They have perfect hair and perfect skin and perfect clothes. If I had any of those things, I'm sure I wouldn't mind all those eyes on me. But today is different. Today I'm wearing my new top I got at the mall.

As soon as I saw it on the rack, I knew we were meant to be together. The soft, clingy fabric. The soothing sky-blue color. The low cut that wasn't low enough to get me sent to the principal's office. I even had some bangles painted with sky-blue and violet flowers that Sherae gave me to go with it. And I'm wearing my jeans that actually fit.

I hover outside Spanish. Mrs. Yuknis is saying how a bunch of people didn't do their homework and so we can't do the activity she had planned. Or something like that. My Spanish skills really are lacking.

I go in. Everyone stares.

Including Julian.

Mrs. Yuknis comes over. I give her my late pass.

"¿Tiene la tarea?"

I admit that I don't have my homework.

"*¿No? ¿Por qué no?*"

Somehow I think *Because I didn't feel like doing it* isn't a good enough reason.

Eyes are still on me. I'm still standing in front of the whole class like Exhibit A of a dork display.

Mrs. Yuknis goes off on a tirade about how it's only April and we need to stop acting like the year is already over and get off our lazy butts and do our homework. Or something like that. Of course I had to come in late on the day she's having a snit fit.

I can feel Julian's eyes on me.

I take my time walking to my desk. Then I turn slowly before sitting down so Julian can see the way this top clings to my curves. Not that I have major curves. But at least now he can see that I have some.

I spend the entire class hoping that Julian will come up to me after. When the bell rings, I put my things away slowly.

"Hey," Julian says.

"Hey." I can feel the heat of him next to me. I have no idea what is preventing my desk from bursting into flames.

"You look nice."

I look up at him. How many times have I looked up at Julian like this, with him so patiently by my side? Why is he even talking to me? I totally rejected him. It's like nothing fazes this boy.

"Thanks," I say.

"New shirt?"

"Yeah."

"I thought so."

I get up and sling my bag over my shoulder. My shirt rides up. I tug it down. It clings to my breasts. Which seemed like a good idea in the dressing room. But now I'm embarrassed.

Julian and I are like two inches apart. I can feel him breathing. I can also feel him looking at me. I can only look at the floor.

"Can I get by?" a girl coming in for the next class says. We're blocking the aisle.

Julian touches my arm. He guides me to the door. I let him walk with me touching my arm for the nine steps it takes to get to the door. They are quite possibly the most daring nine steps I've ever taken.

"See you later," he says.

"Yeah. Later."

When Julian walks away from me, all I can think about is getting close to him again.

◆   ◆   ◆

I triumphantly stride past the cafeteria on my way to lit mag. I even give it the finger. Well, I give the wall the finger. Doing it in the doorway would be a bad idea. With my luck, Warner Talbot would see and think I'm giving him the finger.

There are two girls working at computers in the lit mag office. I think one's a sophomore. She doesn't look up from her screen. The other girl is Darby. I've never really talked to her outside of class. She seems like a loner. So she totally catches me off guard by smiling right at me.

"Hey, Noelle," she says. "Congrats on the coeditor gig."

"Thanks."

"How are you liking it?"

"It's good." I'm not about to admit that I'm only here to get out of lunch. Actually, it's not as bad as I expected. Some parts are even fun, like getting my own desk and correcting people's typos. The best part is that it feels really comfortable in here. Like a safe zone.

"Cool," Darby says. "Just let me know if you need anything. I can be found glued to this very station."

I notice Darby's wearing the same shirt I got at the mall a few months ago. Which throws me off all over again. I'm not used to seeing anyone wear the same clothes I do.

"Did you get your shirt at Delia's?" I ask.

"On sale for nine ninety-nine, just the way I like them."

"Me, too."

"Righteous. I hate when I'm stalking something, waiting for it to go on sale but then I panic that they'll sell out, so I buy it anyway and it goes on sale like the next day."

"I know!"

Darby shakes her head. "Tragic," she confirms.

It's so weird how connecting with someone in a different setting can bring out this whole other side of them. Like how certain places inspire us to act in ways we normally wouldn't. If Darby wasn't on lit mag, we'd probably never talk like this.

A pile of submissions to be edited is waiting for me on my desk. Everyone has to hand in a hard copy of their work, then submit a final version by email after they get their edits. There's a Post-it note stuck on top of the pile:

N-
You're a lifesaver.
Rock on.
           -S

I get out a purple pen to edit the first short story. When I'm a teacher, I won't be using red pens to grade papers. Red pens will forever be associated with criticism and bad grades in my mind. I don't want this person to get their short story back with harsh red pen marks all over it. Purple is much friendlier.

I'm on the third page when Simon arrives.

"Lunch!" he announces. He's carrying a tray piled high with good things to eat. Grilled cheese sandwiches, fruit, bottles of water and iced tea, chips, brownies, and cookies. "I got way too much as usual."

"Sweet!" Darby says. "Thanks, Simon."

Simon puts the tray down on the big table in the middle of the office. Darby goes over and takes an apple and a cookie.

Sophomore girl is still oblivious that anyone else is in the room.

"Help yourself," Simon insists. "I usually bring a tray in for whoever wants. So you don't have to worry about missing lunch or anything."

"That's awesome," I say. "Thank you." As usual, I'm starving. The grilled cheese smells so good. And the peanut butter cookies look amazing. It takes a massive amount of restraint to not attack the tray and inhale everything on it.

"I'm a fan of grilled cheese," Simon informs me.

"Same here. But I thought you weren't allowed to take trays out."

"They let me anyway. The older lunch lady likes my ties. And I always bring the trays back after school."

We work. I have a grilled cheese sandwich. I have some grapes. Then I have two cookies. I'm paranoid that everyone will think I'm taking too much. But no one's noticing. They're busy with their own work.

Everyone else leaves a few minutes early. When the bell rings, it's just me, the office, and the lunch leftovers. I shove two bags of chips in my bag. It would be a waste to leave them behind.

◆　◆　◆

Simon's lunch tray was a sharp contrast to our kitchen. The only time we have enough to eat is when mother gets food stamps. But after a week or so, it's back to starvation city.

The first time mother got food stamps, she dragged me to the grocery store with her. It was a little while after we moved into the apartment, so I was twelve or thirteen. I didn't know why she was taking me. She always went shopping alone.

Mother liked to shop at the upscale gourmet grocery store instead of at the more reasonably priced one a few towns over. She was determined to shop where everyone else did. I pushed the cart while mother selected items from the shelves. Elevator music played. Everything was so clean and shiny. Items were neatly lined up on the shelves. Even the floor gleamed, reflecting rows and rows of perfectly packaged food. I watched a lady switch one box of cereal for another just because the first box was slightly dented on top.

Real moms pushed packed shopping carts past us. Their children riding in the shopping-cart seats had bright, colorful toys or beeping devices to keep them entertained.

We went up to the fancy deli counter. The glass display case gleamed under the bright lights as perky Muzak continued to play. Carefully arranged plates of stuffed artichokes and pesto salad and sautéed portobello mushrooms taunted me. Prepared chickens awaited selection. That deli counter was wrong in so many ways. How could tons of styled food be there for anyone who could afford it, while people around the world were dying because they didn't even have clean water?

Moms were stopping to talk with other moms. None of them even said hi to mother. It was like they knew that even though mother was trying to fit in by shopping there, we were still poor. And Poor was a disease you could catch if you got too close.

Mother has this thing where she gets totally fake in front of other people. I call it her Normal Mom Act. She thinks she can trick people into believing that she's a good mom if she acts like she cares. Sometimes people say that we look more like sisters than mother and daughter. Which makes mother get even phonier, pretending she didn't hear them so they have to repeat it. But no one was even giving her a chance to bust out the Normal Mom Act that day. It was like everyone in the grocery store had made a pact to ignore us.

We got to the checkout line. Mother pushed me in front of her. I was sucking on a lollipop and bit down hard on my tongue when she pushed me. She took our items out of the cart one by one, handing them to me to put on the conveyor belt.

When the cart was empty, she moved up near the cashier.

"How's your day going?" she asked him with a bright smile. The Normal Mom Act was in the house.

"All right." He smiled back at her. "How's it treating you?"

"Can't complain," she said. As if she ever stopped complaining.

The cashier scanned our items. Mother was being all flirty with him. Which was creepy because he was clearly in high school. I was relieved he didn't know me.

Mother said something I don't remember. The cashier laughed.

"Your total is seventy-three oh seven," he said.

She gave him some coupons. Except they weren't coupons. The cashier had been smiling at mother. But when he saw what she gave him, his smile instantly vanished.

He looked at me. He looked at her. He looked back at me.

My tongue throbbed where I'd bitten it.

Then the cashier yelled, "Need a manager on four! Food stamps!"

All the moms in the other lanes turned to see who was using food stamps.

Audrey's mom was three lanes over.

I could see a light of recognition in her eyes. This was back when Audrey and I were friends. I could tell her instinct was to come over and say hello.

But she didn't come over. She just turned around like she didn't even know me.

eleven

friday, april 29

(35 days left)

ꟗ try to avoid school bathrooms as much as possible. It's agonizing to be in the bathroom when a bunch of other girls are using it. I really don't need to hear them gossiping with their friends and checking their phones.

One thing about being bullied is that you quickly learn how to avoid the people who make your life miserable. I never use this bathroom. This is the one Carly uses. But if I tried to fight my way up the crowded stairway to the safer bathroom, I'd be late for class.

Of course Carly comes in as I'm washing my hands.

With Audrey.

"Hi, reject," Carly says. "Having a good day?"

A girl I don't know is at the mirror. I'm mortified she's seeing this. I yank a paper towel out and dry my hands, heading for the door.

"What's the rush?" Carly blocks the door.

"I have class." I hate the panicky ache I always get whenever I see Carly. I keep promising myself I won't let her upset me next time. But when next time comes, it's always like the time before.

"You have class? Or you have an ugly bracelet?"

My bracelet is not ugly. It has delicate, transparent beads strung with an elastic. Sherae gave it to me for my birthday last year. She puts together the most amazing gift bags.

"I think she has an ugly bracelet," Audrey chimes in.

They're still blocking the door.

"Excuse me," I say, trying to get by.

"Oh, *excuse* her!" Carly shrieks to Audrey. "Noelle is *so* much better than us! It's beneath her to even be in the same bathroom!"

"At least she's using the bathroom," Audrey says. "Half the chairs in this school are smeared with her blood."

The bell rings. The girl at the mirror hurries out. She throws me a disgusted look.

"Can you guys move?" I ask.

"Sure," Carly says. "How's this?" She gets right in my face, grabs my wrist, and yanks my bracelet off. Then she stretches the elastic like a rubber band and flings it over a stall door.

"Nice one!" Audrey praises. They actually high-five. After they leave, I can still hear them laughing down the hall.

I open the stall door that Carly flung my bracelet over. I scan the floor for those pretty beads. But I don't see them anywhere.

Panic clutches my stomach.

I peek into the toilet. My bracelet is sitting at the bottom.

Part of me wants to take it out, wash it, and put it back on. But even though I love that bracelet, I can't make myself reach into the toilet for it.

It sucks that Carly gets away with stuff like this. And it sucks that Audrey is part of it now.

Audrey and I were best friends back in fifth grade. After we moved out of Lewis's house to our tiny apartment, everything changed. Not overnight. But gradually, mother became more distant. She shut down. She stopped looking at me or talking to me or taking care of me in any real way. And it's been getting worse ever since.

Audrey and I stayed friends after we moved. But everything changed on Valentine's Day when we were thirteen. She was stoked because Corey Smith had given her a big, heart-shaped box of chocolates. She had a massive crush on Corey Smith. Until he gave her the chocolates, she wasn't sure if he liked her back. Audrey had only eaten three pieces. I couldn't figure out how she resisted eating the whole box.

I went over to Audrey's after school. We were playing Sorry! on Audrey's bed when her mom called her down to try on a dress for this wedding she was in.

"Do I have to?" Audrey groaned down to her mom.

"Yes! It needs to be hemmed!"

"Can I do it later? We're in the middle of a game."

"No, I need you down here right now!"

Audrey made a face. "I'll be right back," she told me.

But she didn't come right back. She was down there for a long time. And I was alone with her Valentine's Day chocolates.

I only meant to have one piece. I didn't think Audrey would

care. So I snuck a piece. Then I got *Tiger Eyes* off her bookshelf because she kept telling me I had to read it. I ate another piece of chocolate while I was reading. And another.

The broken version of Mother After Lewis never bought sweets. She thought she was fat. Which was weird because she was so skinny you could totally see her hipbones jutting out. We didn't even have sugar in the kitchen. I craved sugar so much it was ridiculous. I'd never seen a box of chocolates that big. Each one had a different filling and shape and texture. It was like I was in a trance or something, just reading and eating. I really don't know how it happened, but I ended up eating most of the chocolates.

When Audrey came back upstairs, she freaked.

"Who said you could eat my chocolates?"

"I was—"

"Oh my god you ate the whole box!"

"No, I didn't."

"Why did you eat all my chocolates? Who *does* that?"

I had no idea.

"I knew you were jealous Corey liked me, but you didn't have to go and eat all my chocolates!"

"I'm not jealous!"

"If you were happy for me, you wouldn't have eaten my entire Valentine's Day present!"

That was the moment Audrey and I stopped being friends. It wasn't just about me eating her chocolates. I'm sure my other friends were noticing how strange I had become. People were looking at me differently, like I wasn't one of them anymore. Everyone found out I lied about mother. And then Audrey told them about the chocolates. People were telling Audrey that she'd be un-popular if she stayed friends with me.

Audrey took their side. She didn't want to look back on this time in her life as the worst time ever. The way I already know I will.

◆　◆　◆

Top line of a flyer found in the English hallway:

Are You a Team Player?

◆　◆　◆

I'm just minding my own business going to class when I turn a corner and there's Julian.

Talking to Jolene DelMonico.

Gorgeous Jolene DelMonico with her straight, shiny blonde hair.

Jolene leans in close to Julian. Apparently, she's unable to hear what he's saying unless part of her body is touching part of his. She laughs at something he just said, tossing her head back so all of that long, smooth, silky hair swings luxuriously behind her. I've always been jealous of Jolene's hair. But I haven't been insane-ly jealous until now.

Of course Julian is talking to her. Even their names are cute together. Julian and Jolene. Jolene and Julian. Jolian. Maybe he used to like me, but I pushed him away.

Losing the genetic lottery sucks. I'd give anything to look like Jolene. To get up in the morning and not have to worry about what I'm going to do if my skin is all broken out or if my eyes are puffy or how I'm going to make my hair look decent enough to walk out the door. I wish my hair glinted sunlight and moved in the breeze the way Jolene's does.

If I have to endure my spastic hair for one more day, I'm seriously going to lose it.

Sherae thinks she's driving me home after school. But when she comes over to my locker I say, "I really need to go to the mall."

"What for?"

"This." I point at my head.

"Could you be more specific?"

"Hello! My hair? It's ridiculous! I can't stand it anymore!"

"What are you going to do?"

"I don't know yet."

We go to the expensive hair place at the mall. I call it Fancy-cuts. I can never afford to go there. I always get my hair cut at Supercuts. But Sherae's insisting that I borrow money and she won't take no for an answer.

I'm not about to protest.

Sherae leaves to scope out this new book we're dying to read. I get whisked into Fancycuts, then seated at one of the stylist's stations. The counter in front of me has some glossy magazines neatly fanned out and swanky bottled water. They even ask if I want tea.

This is going to be one fierce haircut.

The guy who's about to cut my hair doesn't really speak English. He's not understanding what I want. He gives me a pencil and a piece of paper so I can sketch it for him. Not exactly what I was expecting from the most upscale hair stylists around.

I draw what's supposed to be my profile. I draw my nose really big to make sure he understands it's my nose. I draw my hair straight and ask him to blow it out. Then I try to draw angling on the side with blunt ends, the way Jolene DelMonico's hair is. She has it cut straight across the back with these boxy ends that always make her hair look like it was just trimmed that morning.

My guy nods like he gets what I want.

I sit back. He spritzes my hair. The spritz smells like flowers. I take a big whiff of it. Then I proceed to have a coughing fit. I clearly do not belong here and all these fancy people know it. Trying to blend in, I pick up a glossy magazine and start flipping through it. I hardly ever get to read magazines. Being decadent for a change will be fun.

When my guy tells me he's done, I wish I had more time. I really want to finish this article about a girl who got plastic surgery so people would stop bullying her. But I'm excited to see my new upscale haircut with professional angling and blunt ends. It should look like a shorter version of Jolene's.

Except that's not what I see. Not even close.

What I see is the worst haircut in the history of the world. This butcher destroyed my hair so badly I can't believe I'm looking in the right mirror. Huge chunks of hair around my face have been chopped off. He didn't cut the sides at an angle. He cut stairs into the sides of my head.

This isn't a haircut. It's a staircut.

I. Am. *Mortified.*

I stay frozen in my chair. My eyes get watery. It takes all the effort I can manage not to burst into tears.

The staircutter is asking what I think. I want to yell at him so bad. I want to storm out without paying. Instead, I don't say anything. I get out of the chair. I hand over Sherae's money and go wait for her outside.

When Sherae shows up, one look at her face confirms what I already know.

"It's really bad, right?" I ask.

Sherae shakes her head slowly. "No, it's . . . not that bad." But the horror in her eyes confirms it's a disaster.

"What am I supposed to do now?" I panic. "There's no way I can go to school like this."

All I want to do is go home and hide, but I let Sherae drag me to Claire's. She picks out a bunch of hair clips and pins for me. My eyes keep getting blurry. I blink back tears, determined not to cry in front of her. At least I have the weekend to figure this out. There has to be some way to make my hair look decent.

◆   ◆   ◆

There is no way to make my hair look decent.

The first thing I do when Sherae drops me off at home is go to my room and cry. I thought I hated my hair before. But this is so much worse.

After I'm completely dehydrated from crying, I take the hair things Sherae got me at Claire's into the bathroom. I spread the sparkly pins and cute clips out over the counter. It was awesome of Sherae to buy me all this stuff. I don't know what I'd do without her.

I spend the next hour trying out every combination of hair

tools I can imagine. Nothing helps. In the end, I settle for pinning the top two steps of my staircut with bobby pins so they're overlapping the bottom step. It sort of looks like I'm just wearing my hair back. Or maybe it looks like I'm the biggest reject ever.

I'm whipped up into a froth of agony by the time mother gets home. She scavenges through the kitchen cabinets, hunting for random scraps to scrape together for dinner. I don't know why she's bothering. There's never anything to eat. We have some stale crackers. Some odd spices that were here when we moved in. A lonely packet of revolting mint hot-chocolate mix. She should throw those things out. But clinging to them gives her backup when she insists there's stuff to eat.

She opens the refrigerator. Which is an even bigger joke. The entire contents of our refrigerator are a jar of spicy mustard, butter, and the end piece of a loaf of bread.

"You ate the rest of the cheese?" mother accuses.

"There wasn't anything else to eat. And it wasn't even that much."

"I can't keep food in the house if you're going to gobble everything up in one day."

"Um, it's called I'm hungry?"

My stomach growls loudly. She can't pretend she doesn't hear it.

"There's never anything to eat!" I yell at her.

Mother looks up from where she's crouched in front of the refrigerator. "Excuse me?" she says.

This could be dangerous. When mother's in a bad mood that isn't my fault, she'll rant about her job even more than usual.

Or she'll sit around staring into space, playing her sad music. If I'm lucky, she'll go hide out in her room so I won't have to deal with her. But when I'm the one who made her angry, she'll get crazy nasty for days and do scary things like slam my door in the middle of the night. I hate being on edge, carrying that nervous feeling around in my stomach of never knowing what to expect. I'm nervous all day at school. I really don't need to be nervous at home, too. I should just stay quiet.

Except I'm not thinking rationally right now.

"There's never anything to eat," I say. "Isn't it against the law to starve your kid?"

Mother scoffs. "You're far from starving."

"Why, because I'm not anorexic like you? Because I actually worry about not getting any nutrients? It's normal to want three meals a day." I'm craving the kind of dinner Mrs. Feldman makes so badly I can't stand it. Delicious main dish. Pretty bowls of side dishes. Basket of warm, homemade bread with whipped butter. The wanting is driving me crazy.

Mother closes the refrigerator door. "I can't deal with the grocery store tonight. Guess I'll run to McDonald's."

"Why can't we ever have real food?"

"Real food costs money. McDonald's has a Dollar Menu. Guess which we can afford?"

I hate that she's right. How ridiculous is it that fresh produce is so expensive? Shouldn't food that's good for you be affordable and junk food cost more?

Mother gets back from McDonald's a thousand years later. She takes cheeseburgers and fries out of the bag. I'm so hungry I don't even care what I'm eating. I stuff my mouth with huge bites of burger. I cram in fries.

Then I start crying.

I should not be forced to eat this crap.

I bat my fry carton across the table. I'm disgusted by everything right now.

"You shouldn't be feeding me this junk," I say. I wipe my eyes with the thin napkin. It rips apart on my face. "We should be eating healthy food. Why am I the one explaining this to you? *You're* supposed to be the mother!"

Instead of waiting to see how angry she'll get, I storm off to my room. I slam the door. Let her be the scared one this time.

She never even noticed my hair. I can't remember the last time she really looked at me.

I have this fantasy of going to Retail Rodeo one day when mother's working. I'd pile my basket full of all the things I need that she never buys me, like deodorant and face cleaner and tampons. Then I'd go over to customer service, ring that stupid bell they have on the counter, and drop my basket in front of mother when she comes out.

"I would like a refund," I'd say, "on a defective mother. And P.S.? Here are some of the things I need. I'm a teenage girl, in case you haven't noticed."

It would be epic. I just wish I had the courage to actually do it.

Parents should be interviewed before they're allowed to have kids. They interview people to work at McDonald's. Isn't taking care of a kid a way more important job?

Sometimes I wonder if things would be different if my parents were married. The only thing I know about my father is that he's an addict. He left when I was one. But then a few years later, he came back. He must have been high that day. He came bursting into Lewis's house threatening mother that if she wouldn't let him see me, he'd take me away.

That's all I remember. He went away again and never came back.

Being a parent isn't supposed to be a job you can quit.

twelve

(34 days left)

Warner Talbot takes one look at me in physics.

"Nice hair," he announces.

"What did she *do*?" Jolene DelMonico wonders.

Welcome to my Monday.

◆　◆　◆

I concentrate on avoiding Julian between classes. There's no way I can face him with my hair like this. Matt probably wouldn't be too bothered, but I tell him that I can't hook up today because I have to do some homework in study hall.

When it's time for Spanish, I dart in with my head down. I put my hand up to cover the side of my hair facing Julian, pretending that I'm smoothing it. I can tell Julian's already here without having to look up. It's like there's this force field around him that I can always detect when he's nearby. I slide into my seat. My plan is to quietly start getting my stuff together before the bell rings so I can run out. If I do this every day until my hair grows out, maybe Julian won't notice that I'm more deformed than ever.

My plan to make a fast exit backfires. Mrs. Yuknis slams us with a pop quiz ten minutes before the end of class. I'm still answering the last question when the bell rings. I pass my quiz up and prepare to bolt.

Julian is right by my desk.

"I like your hair like that," he says.

"Yeah, right," I mumble. It's bad enough being inflicted with a staircut. Does he really have to make fun of me like everyone else?

"I'm serious. It looks nice pulled back. You can see your face more."

I peek up at him. He doesn't appear to be making fun of me.

"Oh. Well . . . thanks." Julian probably feels bad for me. There's no way I can compete with Jolene. I don't know why I even tried.

◆　◆　◆

Gym. Shoot me now.

We're playing volleyball today. Volleyball ranks extremely high on my Worst Things We Have to Play in Gym list. The only thing worse than volleyball is dodgeball. Dodgeball isn't remotely a good idea. Since when does a bunch of balls being hurled at you sound like fun? Why is that even allowed? Volleyball is almost as excruciating. Instead of balls being whipped at you from all directions, one ball fired right at you instigates the inevitable disappointment of everyone on your team when you can't smack it back.

Any time balls are flying at me, I'm an unhappy girl.

Pretty Perfect Popular girls are picking teams. Triple Ps always get to pick teams. They are the Deciders.

I am always their last choice.

We gather in a clump across from the Deciders. The polished gym floor has all these lines painted on it. I have no idea what any of them mean.

"Jolene," Caitlin Holt says.

Jolene DelMonico whisks herself over to the Other Side. Once you are on the Other Side, you are safe.

The Deciders go back and forth, selecting who gets to cross over. Rewarding all the other girls who were born beautiful. Confirming the genetic lottery losers.

"Kim," Caitlin Holt says.

The teams get bigger. Our clump gets smaller.

I always promise myself that I won't get upset next time we're picking teams. And then it's next time and everyone's smirking at me from the Other Side and I'm a sweaty, dizzy mess all over again.

Only three of us remain in the clump.

"Noelle," Caitlin Holt relents.

I cross the divide on shaky legs. There is no walk of shame more shameful than this one.

Caitlin Holt only picked me because she had to. I wish someone would pick me because they want to.

◆　◆　◆

After carving out a squiggle for my new mobile and painting it lime green, it's time to chill with my people on *Friday Night*

Lights. My shows and books are an instant mood adjuster. They're my drugs of choice. And the fictional characters I love are like my friends.

My stomach clenches when I hear mother's car pulling into the driveway. The warm, fuzzy feeling I had going is erased in one harsh swipe. I get tense like this every night when she comes home. But her weird behavior since the McDonald's Incident is making my stomach hurt even more.

All mother did the whole weekend was sit around sulking. She'd either hide out in her room or sit on the couch, staring at nothing for hours. I knew there'd be fallout from yelling at her, but it was ridiculous. Mother hogged the living room last night. She planted herself on the couch, cranked up her oldies, and just spaced out.

I was trying to do my homework. Which was impossible with her annoying music blasting through the cardboard wall. Her music was so loud that it sounded like she'd come into my room and cranked my stereo instead. Focusing on my Spanish essay was impossible. So I went into the living room. Mother was still lost in her own world on the couch.

"Could you turn that down?" I yelled over the music. "Some of us are trying to do homework."

Mother ignored me.

"You have to turn it down!" I yelled louder.

She glared at me. A scary, hateful glare. Like I was the enemy. Which mother had already made clear. I'd heard the diatribe a thousand times. If it wasn't for me, mother would be happy and married and wouldn't have to work at a job she hates. I've ruined her life by existing.

She didn't move from the couch. I stomped over to the stereo and poked the OFF button.

"You have to let me concentrate," I said. "A person should be allowed to do her homework." I was the first person in the history of public education begging to do homework on a Sunday night.

There hasn't been any drama tonight. Even more perplexing is mother's anomalous good mood. We're actually sitting here having dinner without her verbal vomit contaminating everything.

"Eat your carrots," she says. Why is she trying to bust out the Normal Mom Act when no one else is here?

"Carrot cubes are not real carrots," I object.

"Sure they are."

"They don't even taste like carrots. And I'm pretty sure carrots don't come in neon orange. These might be radioactive." I don't think mother knows how to prepare a vegetable that doesn't come from a can. She even manages to mess those up.

"Eat them anyway," she says like we're sharing an inside joke.

Beyond irritating.

I swear, when she gets fake like this, it's even more annoying than her usual stank mood. At least then I know she's for real.

thirteen

tuesday, may 3

(33 days left)

$\mathcal{M}$att's already waiting for me when I get to our place.

"You look different," he says.

Is he seriously just noticing my hair now? I mean, we haven't hooked up since last week, but still. He sees me in the halls. He's had plenty of chances to notice.

"Don't remind me," I grumble.

"No, you look good. But . . . what's different?"

Wait. He doesn't even know it's my hair? Does he not see that half of it was chopped off and it's all pinned back?

"You can't tell?" I ask.

Matt pulls me close to him. "I can tell you're pretty," he whispers. Then he kisses me.

I let myself be kissed. Pretty soon I forget that there's anything to be mad about.

"Oh my god, it's *true*?" a girl's voice yells from behind the wall.

A girl's voice I recognize.

Because she used to be my best friend.

Audrey stomps over to us. She has crazy eyes. "Carly told me you guys came out here, but I had to see for myself."

"We're not—this isn't how it looks," Matt protests.

"Oh, no? Then why does it look like my boyfriend was just kissing a dirty skank?"

I gape at Matt. He's Audrey's *boyfriend*? How can he be her boyfriend when he's *my* boyfriend?

Matt's not explaining that this is all a joke. Or that Audrey is lying. He's not even looking at me.

"How many times have you guys come out here?" Audrey wants to know.

"It's not a big deal," Matt says. "She's not even—"

"How *many*?!"

"I don't know."

"More than twice?"

"Yeah, but—"

"Asshole!"

"Audrey, come on." Matt touches Audrey's arm. It's like I'm not even here. All Matt cares about is convincing Audrey that I'm nothing.

"Don't *touch* me!"

"I—"

"Get off me!" Audrey shakes Matt off. She gives me such a nasty look that I can't believe we were ever best friends.

"First Corey, and now this?" she accuses me.

Is she really bringing up those Valentine's Day chocolates Corey Smith gave her in eighth grade?

"I wasn't jealous of Corey. And I didn't even know you were . . ." My throat gets tight.

"That I was *what*?"

"Going out with . . . Matt."

"Yeah right, I'm sure you didn't."

"I didn't!"

"Gee, I wonder why I don't believe you."

"Tell her I didn't know!" I yell at Matt.

"Like I'm really going to trust you guys." Audrey's glare is ice-cold. "This isn't over," she threatens. Then she storms off.

"Why—" I start to ask Matt. But he runs after Audrey, leaving me behind.

◆　◆　◆

"What just happened?" Sherae says.

"You heard *already*?"

"Everyone's talking about it." Sherae glances back at the cafeteria. After Matt abandoned me, I stayed out at our place until Spanish started. No way was I going to class. I could feel how puffy my eyes were from crying. I couldn't stop shaking. Sherae has lunch fourth period, so I snuck over to the cafeteria and waved her out.

"They are?" I say.

Sherae looks at me. "No, not *everyone*," she backtracks. "Just . . . some people heard from Audrey."

"Heard what?"

"You know Audrey. She's saying you stole Matt from her or some such nonsense."

"I didn't even know they were going out!"

"Are you going to tell me what happened?"

I tell her everything. The words squish my heart like a sponge. Then the tears come back in a rush.

"Here." Sherae brings me down the hall a little. We sit against the wall.

When I can talk again, I say, "I thought Matt and I could be together for real. I thought if I just gave him more time, he'd realize that he loves me. And that he'd want everyone to know we're together." I wipe my eyes with the back of my hand. "He said he wanted to be with me. He said he cared about me. He was the only one who could be my boyfriend and now he's gone. I just can't believe—"

"Where are you girls supposed to be?" a security officer interrupts.

"Lunch," Sherae tells him.

"Both of you?"

"Yes." She grabs my arm. "We're going in."

We might have gotten away with it if the lunch monitor wasn't one of those annoying people who remember every little thing.

"Haven't seen you in a while," he informs me, blocking the door.

"Yeah, I have lit mag now."

"Fifth period?"

"Yeah."

"This is fourth."

Man, he's good.

I tell Sherae I'll meet her at her locker before fifth. Then I sneak down to the bathroom I used to hide out in. I was hoping that I wouldn't ever have to hide in there again. But that's the thing about life. You can never trade yours in for a better one.

◆　◆　◆

Note about Noelle Wexler found on the floor of biology class in ninth grade, written on wide-ruled binder paper in alternating pink and blue ink:

> *Is NW wearing two shirts?!*
> I think she has a leotard on.
> *Why can't you ever see her bra straps?*
> She never wears a bra.
> *Ew. Tacky much?*
> She probably thinks it's attractive.
> *Slut alert!*

◆　◆　◆

Of course the whole school knows by the end of the day.

Including Julian.

I wonder which version of the rumor he heard. Probably the one where Matt and I were doing it in the middle of the tennis court.

When Julian finds me at my locker after school, I don't even try to escape. I just hope this part of the truth will make him feel better.

"Guess what I heard," he says.

"How many guesses do I get?"

"Is any of it true?"

"What did you hear?"

"That you were going out with Matt Brennan."

"Then I guess you heard right."

"I didn't know you had a boyfriend."

"No one did."

"Why didn't you tell me?"

"I'm sorry. It's complicated."

Julian shakes his head.

I wait. I don't know what to say.

"Whatever," Julian says.

For the second time today, I watch a boy I love walk away from me.

Matt wasn't the only reason I can't be with Julian. But it's easier to let him think it was.

fourteen

wednesday, may 4

(32 days left)

When your heart is shattered into a million pieces, all you can do is try to keep holding on. You breathe. You try to fall asleep. You try to not think about him.

Last night was a million years long. I kept looking at the clock, willing it to be morning already. I even thought about taking out my secret box.

I drag myself to the bus stop. All I wanted to do was stay in bed. I was going to tell mother I was sick, but she goes ballistic if I'm still home when she wakes up.

I'm waiting for the stupid bus when a car pulls up to the curb. I hardly notice it at first, assuming it's just one of the moms dropping her kid off. But then I see who's in the car.

It's Audrey. With her friends.

This is not good.

"Hey, scuzball!" Audrey yells.

All the kids at the bus stop stare at me.

"What kind of loser takes the bus when they're old enough to drive?" she speculates.

I kind of have to agree with her on that one.

The kids standing closest to me back a few steps away. Everyone knows that Loser is catching.

The car squeals away. For the first time in my life, I can't wait for the bus to get here. It picked the worst possible day to be late.

A minute later, another car turns down the street. Except it's not another car. It's the same car with Audrey and her friends.

As the car gets closer, I realize that they're all holding shotguns.

This is it.

They're going to kill me.

I can't believe this is how it all ends. On a gorgeous spring day under an impossibly blue sky, waiting for the bus.

Unreal.

Audrey leans out the back window. She positions the gun on her shoulder. She targets me through the viewfinder.

Everyone at the bus stop runs.

I should be running, too. I tell myself to run. But really, what's the point? When I'm dead, I won't have to endure this relentless pain. Maybe I'll come back as a kid with a better life. Or maybe I'll pass over into that alternate universe where outsiders don't even exist.

So I stand there. Looking straight at Audrey. Daring her to do it.

The first impact hits me in the stomach. Someone screams. I

look down at myself. There's a splatter of red on my shirt. More splatters start showing up on my arms. I put my hands over my head and crouch down. I hear the car zoom by.

When it sounds like the car is gone, I slowly take my hands away and look up. One of the middle school girls is crouched behind a tree, crying as her friend hugs her. A freshman boy runs over to me.

"Are you okay?" he asks.

That's a good question. Shouldn't I be dead by now? Red is splattered all over me. Some of the places where I got hit really sting.

"Those paintballs can be rough," he says.

Paintballs? They shot me with *paintballs*? Those guns looked *real*.

"I'm okay," I tell him. "But I should probably go home and change."

"Good thing you crouched down. It could have been a lot worse if they hit you in the face."

I'm a trembling wreck going home. I try to wipe some paint off my arm where it stings the worst. The red paintblood smears.

My key shakes when I try to put it in the lock. There's a good chance I might throw up. I try not to wake up mother as I go to my room and close the door. My shirt is ruined. And of course I had to be wearing my only jeans that fit. I take everything off, careful not to get paint on the carpet.

Mother bangs on my door.

"Just a minute," I say.

"What are you doing home?" she demands through the door.

"Can you give me a minute?" I yell. I put on a fresh shirt and jeans and open the door.

"Why are you here?" mother says.

"I had to change my clothes."

"Why?"

I kick my splattered jeans and shirt over to her.

"What happened?" she asks. "What's this all over your clothes?"

"I was waiting for the bus and—" My throat closes up.

I will not cry about this. Not now.

"Some kids shot paintballs at me," I manage to whisper.

"Are you okay?"

Am I *okay*? Since when does mother care if I'm okay? She even looks concerned like a real mom.

"It hurts," I say.

"Go to the nurse when you get to school."

"I missed the bus. Can you drive me?"

Mother never drives me to school. She always makes me walk the mile to the train station, even when it's freezing out. But today should be different.

She takes another look at my arms. I watch the concern in her eyes fade to disinterest.

"I can't be late today," she says. "You can take the train."

◆ ◆ ◆

Physics is almost over by the time I get there. Everyone's doing an activity in groups. I give my late pass to Ms. Scofield. She looks like she wants to say something, but she just tells me to join my group.

I slog over to my desk and put my bag down. I don't bother to take anything out. I slide my desk closer to Ali's, but I don't ask what the activity is. I don't care about anything. I just want to go home.

"Are you okay?" Ali asks.

Just her asking if I'm okay makes me want to burst out crying. I blink back tears. I don't want anyone to see me like this. I don't want it to get back to Audrey that she made me cry in class.

I glance at the other two kids in our group. They're oblivious, arguing over something on the activity sheet.

"Did they hurt you?"

"Who?"

"Audrey. And her friends. I heard about what happened."

"You heard *already*?" How is that even possible? Did Audrey hijack the PA system and make an announcement during homeroom?

"Someone was talking about it before class."

"Who?"

"Do you really have to ask?"

I look at Warner's group. He catches me looking. He holds out his hand like a gun and shoots it.

Pow, he mouths.

He probably wishes I were dead. But then he wouldn't have anyone to make fun of anymore. Except Ali. And Tommy. And maybe some dorky freshmen.

"Do you want to come over after school?" Ali offers. I'm sure she recognizes her own pain in my eyes. "We could make smoothies and watch a movie. That always takes my mind off things."

"I can't," I say. "But thanks." I just want to be alone. I hate everyone.

When the bell rings, I grab my bag and dash for the door. Simon catches up to me. He doesn't say anything. He just puts his arm around me and walks me to my locker. Sherae's waiting there for me. She exchanges a look with Simon. I should be protesting that I don't need babysitters, but I don't care. I am officially over everyone and everything.

"See you at lit mag?" Simon asks me.

I nod at the floor.

The bell rings. The halls empty out. I don't move. Neither does Sherae.

"Those look like they hurt," she says. She means the red welts on my arms. A few of them are turning into nasty bruises.

"I guess."

"Let's go to the nurse."

"I'm okay."

"I'm not convinced."

"I am."

"Why don't we let the nurse decide?"

I'm too tired to fight. So I let Sherae take me to the nurse's office. The nurse sends Sherae to class. Then she asks me what happened.

"I got hit with paintballs."

"When?"

"Before school. At the bus stop."

She inspects my arms.

"Who did this to you?" she wants to know.

If I tell the nurse it was Audrey, she'll tell the principal and Audrey will get in trouble. Which will motivate her to make my life an even bigger nightmare. I'd rather lay low and wait for this to blow over.

"It doesn't matter," I say.

The nurse is radiating so much concern that I have to look away. She has pictures of a little girl on her desk. I bet she's an amazing mom.

I blink back tears again. My whole life is blinking back tears. It's getting really old.

"You're okay," she says. "You'll be good as new. Sit here for me?"

I sit on the patient table. The white paper sheet crinkles under me.

"Can you lift up your shirt?"

"Why?"

"I want to check the other bruises."

When I lift my shirt, her expression shifts. It's only for a second. Then she's smiling again and putting on ointment and explaining that my bruises should go away soon. I won't even know they were there.

I wish emotional bruises healed like physical ones.

fifteen

thursday, may 5

(31 days left)

Lit mag. My salvation. It's the one place at school where I can relax, even if other kids are working in here with me. I've gotten to know everyone. They're a cool group. Plus, I'm actually more interested in writing and editing than I thought I was. Making things happen behind the scenes of a publication, even our small-town lit mag, is kind of cool.

"Lunch is served," Simon announces. He puts his tray on the big table. The smell of fried chicken makes me happy.

Today it's just me and Simon. These are the best times. Simon is so easy to talk to. Sometimes it feels like I could open up to him about anything and he'd totally understand. Even though his family is crazy wealthy, he's not conceited at all. He's one of the few kids around here who hasn't been brainwashed by excessive privilege. High school would be a piece of cake if everyone were like Simon.

"You're too good to me," I say.

"Nope, just hungry. Come eat."

"In a minute. I have to finish these edits."

"Later. Your fried chicken is getting cold. And I got extra-crispy pieces."

Extra-crispy fried chicken is what's up. I sit across from Simon and take a plate of fried chicken, mashed potatoes, and green beans. Everything looks so good.

For a while we just eat and talk about lit mag stuff. Then Simon asks if I'm okay. My automatic response is that I'm fine. But lying is really exhausting. It would be a relief to be honest with Simon.

"No," I admit. "I'm not okay." I tell him about the whole Matt/Audrey debacle. Then I tell him about Julian.

"Wait," Simon interrupts. "If you want to be with Julian, then why aren't you with him?"

"Seriously?"

"Yeah. It sounds like you're both into each other."

"It's not that simple."

"Why not?"

"I'm . . . not good enough for him."

"*What?* That's ridiculous."

"No, that's how it is."

"Sorry if no one's told you this before, but any guy would be lucky to be with you. You're smart, funny, insightful, talented, caring . . . don't you see any of that?"

Wow. No one's ever said anything like that to me before.

"Well . . . jeez, Simon. Thanks."

"It's the truth. Do yourself a favor and start believing it."

I can't help smiling. Simon can inspire anyone. Maybe he'll be our next great leader in ten years.

"Oh, man." Simon jumps up. "I'm supposed to be showing Mr. Gilford those proofs. You have everything you need?"

"Yeah, I'll just be finishing the edits."

Simon grabs his bag and a folder. Right before he leaves he says, "Hey, Noelle?"

"Yeah?"

"Everything will work out the way it's supposed to."

"I hope so."

The nice things Simon told me nestle into an empty place inside my soul. It's like he really believes everything he said. When I hear someone come into the office a few minutes later, I look up from my work smiling all big, expecting to see Simon.

But it's Carly.

I live in constant fear that Carly will humiliate me in the hall or outside. She owns everywhere else. She's not allowed to invade my one safe place.

"So that thing you did with Matt?" she says. "Wasn't cool."

"You're not supposed to be in here."

"Oh, no?" Carly strides over to my desk. She picks up my supply organizer and turns it over. Pencils, staples, paper clips, and tacks scatter everywhere. She leans down close. "Who's going to stop me?"

The bell never rings when you need it to. The clock says we have six minutes left. My pulse is racing the same way it always does when Carly busts out tormenting me. She is the hunter. I am the wild animal, praying she'll make it quick.

"Leave," I tell her.

"That's not very nice. Kind of like when you skanked around with Matt behind Audrey's back. That wasn't very nice, either, now was it?"

"I didn't know they were going out."

"Yeah . . . no one believes you."

"Why do you even care?"

"Um, because Audrey's my friend? And when people hurt my friends, they hurt me." Carly gives my chair a hard shove. It starts wheeling across the room. I jump off and head for the door. But Carly's right there, grabbing my arm.

"I don't think so," she says.

"Let me go."

"No. I want to show you something."

"Let me *go*!" I yank my arm away.

She grabs me harder and pushes me to the other side of the room. I can't get away from her. She's way stronger than I am. The door is open, though. I could scream until someone comes. But then what would I say? That Carly was grabbing me? Then she'd get in trouble and attack me even harder next time. And everyone would know how weak I am.

No. It's better to just see what she wants. The bell will ring in four minutes and the hall will get crowded and she'll leave me alone.

"Audrey wanted me to give you a message," Carly says.

"What?"

"This." She grabs my hand and yanks on my index finger. My knuckle cracks.

"Ow!"

"Don't be dramatic. It doesn't hurt yet." Carly pushes me over to the paper cutter. She lifts the slicer. Then she presses my finger against the edge of the cutter.

Right below the blade.

"Stop!" I yell, snatching my finger away.

Carly grabs my hair. She pulls it all the way back.

"Let me *go*!" I yell louder. Now I want someone to hear.

No one comes in.

Carly is pulling my hair so hard that I can't look anywhere but at the ceiling. My neck is killing. I try to kick her. I try to shove her away. Nothing works.

"What happened to your hair?" Carly asks. She grabs a piece of my staircut and flips the short section of hair against my face. "Why's it all chopped up?"

Maybe I'd be able to answer if my neck weren't bent all the way back.

"I guess that's how you like it," Carly concludes. "So you won't care if I chop it up some more." She shoves me down over the paper cutter. The side of my head slams against it so hard I hope my brain still works. "Let's see." Carly rips some pins out of my hair. "Which part is too long?"

"Stop it. Let me go."

Carly has my arm pinned behind me. I can't move. She pulls a section of my hair under the slicer. I hear the slicer being lifted and lowered, but not all the way. She lifts and lowers the slicer over and over.

The bell rings.

"Psych!" Carly yells. She lets go of me and heads for the door.

In the doorway, she turns to me and says, "Thanks for playing, Rotten Egg. Let's do it again sometime."

◆ ◆ ◆

Mother stopped doing my laundry in the winter of eighth grade. She never said she wasn't going to do it anymore. She just stopped.

I didn't realize this until one morning when I was getting ready for school. I'd thought mother was going to do laundry the night before. I was expecting to wake up and have clean clothes waiting.

But my dirty clothes were still in the hamper.

I panicked. I had nothing to wear. I only had a few long-sleeved shirts and it was really cold that morning. I often dealt with winter by wearing a tee under a cardigan while everyone else was all cozy in their cashmere sweaters. But I didn't want to do that today. It was too cold. And I'd already worn my only decent sweater twice that week.

I lifted the lid off the hamper. Dirty-clothes smell wafted out. The arm of my turtleneck was wrapped around some pajama bottoms. I took out the turtleneck and sniffed it. It smelled like rotten eggs. There was a slight possibility that I could wash it in the sink, put it in the dryer until wearable, take the train to school, and still make it in time for second period. Only, I'd have to walk in the freezing wind all the way to the train station. And mother would be up by then. She'd yell at me for missing the bus.

I went to my closet to see if a new shirt had magically appeared.

It had not.

I returned to the bathroom and sniffed the turtleneck again. The rotten egg smell seemed to be dissipating. I waved it around a little. I sprayed some Sea Island Cotton body spray on it. If I didn't get too close to anyone, maybe I could pull it off.

So I put the dirty turtleneck on.

Of course Carly came up to me when we got to school. She'd been taunting me at the bus stop. She wasn't done.

I took my coat off and put it in my locker.

"You smell like rotten eggs," Carly said.

"No, I don't."

"Did your nose stop working? Because you totally do."

All I wanted to do was run out of there and take the train home and get in bed and hide under the covers for the rest of the day. But I didn't. I went through the whole day smelling like rotten eggs.

When mother got home that night, I asked her when she was going to do laundry. She said that I was old enough to do my own laundry. She didn't show me how to do it or anything. It was just another one of those things that I was expected to figure out on my own.

I read the directions on the box of Tide. They said to put the clothes in the washing machine, then put the detergent in, then start the wash. They didn't say anything about separating colors from whites. They didn't say anything about how if you use extra detergent because you want your clothes to be extra clean, the powder will streak all over your clothes and they'll come out crusted with lumpy chunks of detergent all over them.

The next day, I went to school in jeans with detergent stains and a long-sleeved tee that used to be white but was now a dingy pinkish color. But at least I didn't smell like rotten eggs. Since then, I've learned how to do laundry. I add detergent to the water before I put the clothes in. I separate the whites from the colors.

Another thing I've learned is that when one problem gets solved, another problem comes barging in right behind it, banging its big Problem Parade drum. Now I have clean clothes. But mother doesn't let me take showers in the morning.

We have two bathrooms. You know your town is upscale when even the crappy apartments have two bathrooms. Mine only has a toilet (that likes to stop working at the worst times), a sink, and an ancient washer/dryer unit. The other bathroom is attached to mother's room. Of course that's the one with the shower. Mother's argument is that when I take a shower while she's sleeping, it wakes her up. Mother does not enjoy being woken up before 7:45. Which means I have to take showers at night.

I don't want to take showers at night. I want to take showers before school like a normal person.

That time I smelled like rotten eggs was the end of smelling. I refuse to be dirty ever again. I'm obsessive about washing my sheets twice a week and doing laundry way before I run out of anything. And I have a new set of body sprays that Sherae gave me for my birthday, so I can go to school smelling like lavender or lily of the valley every day.

Some mornings I have a fleeting moment of courage. I'll sneak into mother's bathroom, start the shower, and get in real quick. She usually starts yelling at me to turn the water off. I'll pretend I don't hear her, scrubbing as quickly as I can. But most mornings, I grab a fresh washcloth and wash up at my sink.

◆ ◆ ◆

There's no way I'm going to gym after what Carly just did to me. I can't stop shaking.

The tears come when I get to my locker. This time, I let them fall. I'm tired of holding everything in. What's the difference? No one cares anyway. But then Sherae comes up to me. She doesn't say anything. She just hugs me.

All it takes is that small gesture of caring to make me completely break down. I'm bawling like I'll never be able to stop. Because I just realized something.

I didn't run.

When I thought Audrey was going to shoot me with a real gun, I didn't even try to save my life. I just stood there. The promise of relief that death would bring soothed me at that moment.

Something is wrong with me. Something is desperately wrong.

I pull away from Sherae, slamming back against my locker. I let myself sink down to the floor. I'm having one of those embarrassing crying fits where you're clenched in the steel grip of a scary, convulsive attack. I can't stop making these spastic hiccuping noises. I try taking shuddering breaths to slow down the crying, but it won't stop.

People are staring. I don't blame them. Anyone would stare at a crazy girl having a breakdown in the hall.

I hate that the crazy girl is me.

Who doesn't run the other way when she thinks her life is being threatened? Who doesn't fight to stay alive?

Every single day of my life is a fight. But yesterday, I gave up without even trying. I want to keep fighting. I really do. I'm just so tired of how nothing ever gets better.

◆　◆　◆

When they have school shootings on shows or in movies, it's always a boy with the gun.

What makes them think it could never be a girl?

◆　◆　◆

I'm being kidnapped.

Well. Friendnapped is more accurate. After my breakdown, Sherae picked me up and swept me out of school.

"You should go back in," I say. "You're going to get in trouble."

"Do I look like I care?" Sherae guides me out to the student parking lot through the side door. She puts me in her car. "Let's go."

"Seriously," I tell her. "I'm fine. Don't cut because of me."

Sherae is not hearing that. She turns on her car.

"We're going to my house," she says. "Don't bother trying to convince me otherwise."

Mrs. Feldman is home when we get there. I look away so she can't see my face.

"What's wrong?" she says.

"I'll be right back," Sherae tells her. She takes me to her room. She orders me to pick out pajamas. Then she goes to explain to her mom. I'm not sure what she's saying. I swore her to secrecy. How could she possibly explain about Julian and Carly and Matt and Audrey and Warner and mother and everything without specifics? Like, what, "We came home early because Noelle's life sucks?"

All of the clothes in Sherae's pajama drawer are soft and pretty. Yes, she has an entire pajama drawer. I have two pajama bottoms and some worn-out old tees. I select pale pink capris that are soft as butter and a thin white tank top. Then I get changed.

Sherae comes back to her room with provisions. She has an assortment of sweet and salty snacks.

"Here's what we're doing," she says. "We're going to pig out. We're going to watch whatever you want. We are *not* going to waste our time talking about idiots who don't deserve our attention. What is your viewing desire?"

I've seen every *Freaks and Geeks* ep a zillion times. Sherae lets me borrow her box set whenever I want. But that show always makes me feel better. So Sherae and I climb up on her massive bed and commence a *Freaks and Geeks* marathon.

I try not to think about Julian. I really do. But Daniel Desario reminds me of Matt and Nick Andopolis reminds me of Julian. Except Julian's not a pothead like Nick is.

"Why did Matt pick Audrey?" I groan.

"Because he's an idiot," Sherae explains.

"But why didn't he want me?"

"He did. He just didn't want to choose."

"I hate that I wasn't enough for him."

"I don't. This just proves that Matt was totally wrong for you. The right guy would never make you feel this way."

"Like I'll ever meet anyone right for me."

"Have you met Julian?"

"Julian thinks I'm a skank. Julian and the whole rest of the world."

"No, he doesn't. He wants to be with you. And he knows you want to be with him, even if you keep denying it."

"You know it would never work out."

"No, you *think* it would never work out. Julian obviously likes you. A lot. He'd understand."

"He'd be grossed out."

"Not if he wants to be with you. Which he does."

I take another iced animal cookie from the bag.

"Why is it so hard to believe he actually likes you?" Sherae says. She grabs her hot-pink Uglydoll that resembles a possessed rabbit and smacks me with him. "Hello! He asked you *out*! Julian Porter wants to go out with you! How can you not see how major that is?"

I just shrug. Sherae would never understand.

We watch the scene where Nick sings for Lindsay. Life would be so much easier if fictional boys were real.

sixteen

friday, may 6

(30 days left)

Avoiding the cafeteria hasn't only been necessary at lunch. I've been avoiding it before school, too. I do not want to be trapped in there the next time Julian comes in early. You're not supposed to wait outside before school, but they don't have the energy to herd us in this late in the year.

I sit against a tree and take my book out. I can never completely focus on reading at school. Or anything else, really. Part of me is watching out for Julian and Carly and Matt and Audrey and Sherae. Sherae's coming in from the student parking lot. I wave her over.

"Thanks for yesterday," I say. "I seriously needed that."

"Anytime."

"Are you sure your mom wasn't mad?"

"No way! She loves having you over. Even in emergencies."

The wind whips a chunk of my staircut out of its pin. I press my hair back and scrape the pin against my scalp, trying to smash my hair stair down.

"What time is it?" I ask.

"We have"—Sherae checks—"seven more minutes."

"Let's stay out here."

Sherae sits down on the grass next to me and leans back against the tree. In between kids shouting and car doors slamming, I can hear tree leaves rustling. The warm wind feels good. I so don't want to go in.

It's almost time to go in when Hector comes over to us.

"Can I talk to you?" he asks Sherae.

"I don't think so," Sherae says.

"Just two seconds."

Sherae gets up. "We have to go in," she tells Hector. She looks down at me for help.

I get up. We start walking. Hector walks with us.

"Can you leave me alone?" Sherae says.

"Can you let me talk to you?"

We keep walking.

"Hey." Hector grabs Sherae's bag, jerking her to a stop. "Don't be such a bitch. I just want to talk."

"Come on, Noelle." Sherae grabs my hand. We dash ahead.

When Sherae called me that night after Hector left her house, she was crying so hard. It was the first time I'd ever heard her unhinged like that. I'd always assumed Sherae had everything under control. Her life seemed so perfect. Until Hector took it too far. He didn't listen when she told him to stop.

You can't violate someone's trust and expect there to be no consequences.

◆ ◆ ◆

Fridays aren't just regular Fridays in physics. They're Fun Fizzycks Fridays (aka FFF, aka Fun Fridays). Every Fun Fizzycks Friday, Ms. Scofield has a dork-off against her own corniness. On this particular FFF, Ms. Scofield is attempting to set a new world's record for Corniest Physics Teacher Ever.

"Did you know that Roy G. Biv was an actual dude?" Ms. Scofield inquires.

"I don't think that's right," Jolene says. Her hair is so shiny I need sunglasses.

"An actual dude," Ms. Scofield insists, "who had a cat."

"What was the cat's name?" Warner asks.

"CAT."

"He named his cat Cat?"

"Of course." Ms. Scofield writes CAT on the board. "Colors All There. Get it?"

We stare.

"Because Roy G. Biv represents all colors of the visible light spectrum."

We groan.

"Not your best effort, miss," Jolene remarks snottily.

"Oh, am I extra corny today? My bad. It must be all the excitement of Fun Fizzycks Friday."

Warner snorts.

"Moving on!" Ms. Scofield says, unfazed. "What color is Ali's shirt?"

We all look at Ali. Ali turns red.

Darby says "pink" at the same time Simon says "magenta."

"I'd say it's magenta, too," Ms. Scofield agrees. "But the wild thing is? None of us is seeing the exact shade of color as everyone else. We're all seeing that shade of magenta a little bit differently. Depending on where you're sitting and the way light is reflecting off Ali's shirt, every other color in the visible spectrum is being absorbed except for that one particular wavelength of light that is magenta. It's just that we're all perceiving magenta differently."

That's so weird. I always thought everyone was seeing the same colors. I mean, sometimes I think about how I'm seeing things differently from everyone else because I'm the only one looking at everything from my eyes. Every other person in this room is seeing a different configuration of the room. They're seeing me in a way I can't. The more you think about perception like that, the weirder it gets. But I was hoping we could all count on colors to be the same.

"Which means!" Ms. Scofield tings Lloyd. "That no two people can see the world in the same way. No matter what you're looking at, no one is seeing it the same way you are. Fascinating!"

So it's not just about differences in personality and character and beliefs. We all see the world differently on a physical level. Is it such a stretch to conclude that everyone will always have differences and, therefore, we'll never all agree on any one thing?

We have to do an activity in pairs. Ali and I scooch our desks together.

"Aren't you happy you wore that shirt today?" I ask her.

"Extremely. I probably turned as magenta as my shirt."

"No, you didn't," I say. Even though she kind of did.

I go over to the materials bench to get what we need. The activity is on reflection and refraction. I fill a clear carrying container with lenses, prisms, blocks, diffraction gratings, and some of those sample color strips from the paint store. Then I take everything back to Ali.

Working with her shouldn't feel awkward. We're a pair in here by choice and we've done stuff outside of school before. But as she reads the procedure out loud and I set up the materials, I feel guilty. Ali has asked me over a few times this year. But I always tell her I can't. Ali gets bullied way worse than I do. Carly and Warner and those guys would make my life even more of a living nightmare if Ali and I became better friends.

We're finishing the activity when Ms. Scofield yells over everyone that we have five minutes left. As I put our materials back in the container, I'm hoping Ali won't ask me to come over.

"Do you want to do something after school?" she asks.

"I can't. I have plans with Sherae."

"She's awesome. It would be fun to hang out with her sometime."

I know how desperate Ali is for a friend. I know how much it would mean to her. And still I can't go down that road to even more torture.

I really, really hate myself sometimes.

◆　◆　◆

I get nervous when Sherae comes over. I'm always worried that she'll see something I don't want her to. But this is an emergency.

Hector went up to Sherae again after school. She still wouldn't talk to him. He was like, "You can talk to me here or you can talk to me at your house, because that's where I'm going to wait for you." So I said she could come over and hide out for as long as she wanted. We have at least two hours before mother gets home. Even if Sherae is still here by then, it should be okay. Mother usually puts on her Normal Mom Act in front of other people.

My room is Humiliation Central compared to Sherae's. But it's not like we can hang out anywhere else. The living room is grungy and there's a stack of overdue notices from bill collectors on the table. Sherae never cares about my dingy room, though. She gets on my bed and props my pillows up against the wall. I'm relieved that I saved my old floor pillow from when I was little so I have somewhere to sit.

"Why does he keep bothering me?" Sherae says. "Why can't he just leave me alone?"

"Maybe he's afraid you're going to report him."

"According to him, there's nothing to report. He doesn't even know why I'm mad."

"Why don't you tell him?"

"Seriously? He should *know*." Sherae picks up our latest cootie catcher from my night table. She pulls it open to see if I finished it.

"I hate that you have to go through this," I tell her.

"I hate it more." Sherae starts to say something else, but suddenly she's crying. The crying quickly gets worse. I run to the bathroom to see if mother got more tissues. Of course she didn't. But there's a box in her room. I grab it.

I sit on my bed next to Sherae while she cries. I wish I knew how to comfort her. Should I be saying things like, "It will be okay" in a soft voice, like they do in movies? Should I be rubbing her back or something? I never know what to do.

I just sit with her, holding the tissue box.

Sherae needs to know she's not alone. Everything I rehearse saying to her in my head sounds lacking. But there is one thing I could do. I could try to make her feel better about her life by opening up about mine. Maybe if she heard all the things I've been so ashamed to admit, she'd feel less alone. And the truth is, the pressure of hiding everything from my best friend is crushing me. I want to tell her everything. I *need* to tell her everything.

"This might make you feel better," I begin.

◆　◆　◆

When mother comes home, she doesn't even bother putting on her Normal Mom Act. It's like she somehow knows I've just spent the last hour telling Sherae every nasty thing about her.

"Are those my tissues?" mother accuses.

"We needed them," I retaliate. It's so stupid that I even have to explain about a box of tissues. Shouldn't they be *our* tissues? How messed up is it that the woman hoards basic household supplies?

They say that parents should be role models. That you should look up to them and follow their example of who to be.

I use mother as an example of who *not* to be.

Sherae stopped crying a long time ago. She's looking at mother flatly.

"I'm not cooking," mother broadcasts like this is an unprecedented event. "You girls can make yourselves something if you want."

I love the "if you want" part. Like, you know, just in case you might want dinner tonight. You can make something. In our kitchen that has no food.

"Actually?" Sherae says. "We were just leaving. Come on, Noelle."

This is news to me.

Sherae drives us to our favorite diner. I love it here. The old-school neon signs for the Carnegie Deli and Hostess CupCakes and The Donut Pub. The constant flux of strangers who never judge us. Even the floor tiles are cool. Maybe if every night were Fun Diner Night the whole school thing would be remotely tolerable.

Right after we score our usual window booth, I notice the old lady who's always here, eating her cantaloupe. She's always at a two-seater booth. She's always alone. And she always gets half a cantaloupe. I've heard her ordering it before. She's very particular. Her cantaloupe must meet certain color and firmness criteria. She always looks relieved when the cantaloupe arrives. As if maybe the waitress is going to come back and report that a random hooligan just snatched the last one.

Is that what life comes down to after all your friends have died and your kids are far away living their own lives? Sitting all alone in a diner, eating cantaloupe?

I am so, so thankful that I have Sherae.

We decide that we're starving and must get vast quantities of food. We order club sandwiches with about ten million sides.

Sherae insists she's treating. I'll totally surprise her next time by being the one to treat.

"I'm glad you told me about your mom and everything," she says.

"I should have told you a long time ago. It's just . . . so humiliating."

The waitress puts our drinks in front of us. I say thank you.

"Were you surprised?" I ask Sherae.

"By what you told me?"

I nod, sipping my cherry soda.

"Mostly, yeah. But I already knew some of it."

"Like what?"

"Well . . . I didn't know your mom was insane about laundry, but I knew you ran out of socks a lot."

"Is that why you put those rainbow stripy socks in my gift bag for my birthday?" A bus boy (actually a middle-aged dude) passes by with a pile of plates. He drops a fork. I pick it up for him.

"It just seemed like you needed more socks. Now I know why."

Before I can ask what else she knew, I stop myself. It doesn't really matter. What matters is that Sherae knew more than I thought. Now I realize that she's been doing little things all along to help me without being obvious about it. When I thought she was giving me her old laptop and printer because she got new ones for Christmas, she was actually trying to help me. I guess there are some things you just can't cover up. No matter how hard you try.

Our plates and baskets of food arrive. We forget to talk for a minute. Emotional exhaustion always makes us hungry.

"I can't believe the way your mom treats you," Sherae says. "I'm so sorry she's like that. If my mom treated me that way, I'd hate her."

It's such a relief that Sherae understands. Everyone says how it's impossible to hate your mother. They're all, *But she's your mother.* Like that's supposed to mean something. And maybe it should. But when a parent isn't taking care of you, I think you get to choose what your relationship will become. You can choose to be suffocated. Or you can find a way to keep breathing.

It's cake time. Sherae and I always get cake and coffee for dessert at the diner. But they're out of the cake we like. We consider pie instead.

The waitress shakes her head at this. She leans in conspiratorially.

"Get the coffee cake," she advises. "It's fresh."

"Sold," Sherae says.

"Hey," I go. "We're not just having coffee and cake. We're having coffee cake!"

This cracks us up for no reason. We have successfully transitioned the Worst Day Ever into Fun Diner Night. We rule.

seventeen

monday, may 9

(29 days left)

Banner in main hallway, metallic red with blue lettering:

WE ARE WHAT WE THINK. —BUDDHA

◆ ◆ ◆

Why does gym always have to come along and ruin everything?

My day was actually looking up. Simon brought his usual packed lunch tray to lit mag for everyone, but we were the only ones there. I didn't have to share the mac and cheese or anything else. I even forgot about my hair for five minutes.

And then. Gym happened. Along with the announcement that we're playing volleyball again. But first we have to deal with the warm-up, crunches, and whatever additional horrors Ms. Kane cares to inflict.

Ms. Kane is a tyrant. She's one of those teachers who takes

their problems out on you. She always has something nasty to say and she won't hesitate to tell you that your form sucks. It's obvious she's having a bad day because she's being even more boot camp about form than usual.

"Shoulders up!" she shouts.

As if crunches weren't hard enough without some maniac yelling at us.

"Get those shoulders off the floor!" she shouts louder.

I'm dying. We all are. We've already done way more crunches than we normally do. My abs are on fire.

"Push-ups!" Ms. Kane demands.

We flip over and crawl into position.

"I'll wait," Ms. Kane says. She's standing at the front with her hands on her hips, rolling her eyes at the ceiling.

We stay bent over in push-up position, waiting for whoever she's waiting for.

"Still waiting," she says.

I look around to see who she means. Kim Reynolds is not in correct push-up position. She's kneeling instead of balancing on her knees with her hands splayed out on the floor in front of her.

Kim sees me looking at her. "Who's she waiting for?" she mouths.

"I think . . . you," I mouth back.

"What?" Kim looks over at Ms. Kane. Ms. Kane is staring right at her.

"Any day now, Ms. Reynolds," she tells Kim.

"Aw, *hell* no." Kim gets up and strides toward the back door.

"Get back here!" Ms. Kane yells after her.

Kim keeps going. She slams out. She's going to get in major trouble. But it's good to know that some people are strong enough to take a stand against their bullies.

◆ ◆ ◆

Sherae is giving me a ride home. I pick the music while she maneuvers her car in line to pull out of the parking lot. There's always a traffic jam right after school. Cars are clogging the only exit from like five different directions. They should have made another way out.

"If we added up how much time we spend waiting to leave, it would be days," I estimate. "Weeks, even. Weeks of our lives wasted in line."

Sherae isn't listening. She's flashing a glare at the rearview mirror. I turn around to see who she's looking at.

Hector's car is right behind us.

Sherae hurls her door open, jumps out, and slams it.

This. Could be a problem.

She stomps over to Hector's car. He opens his door to get out, but she blocks him.

I turn off the music.

"Do you really not know why I'm mad?" Sherae throws down. Our windows are both open. I can hear everything.

"Not so much," Hector says.

"How could you not know what you did?"

"I've asked you what I did! You won't tell me."

"I shouldn't have to tell you. You were there."

"Can you let me out?"

"Why should I?" Sherae doesn't move. "Why should I do anything you want? You didn't do what I wanted."

"What are you talking about?"

"You took it too far. I told you to stop and you didn't. Ring any bells?"

"I thought you were playing."

"No, I wasn't *playing*. I was trying to keep my virginity. You should have respected that."

"I respect you."

"Forcing me to have sex when I told you I wasn't ready is *dis*-respecting."

"Then why'd you stop saying no?"

Angry cars behind Hector are honking. Hector gets out and waves them around. Then he guides Sherae over behind her car.

"I wasn't ready," she says. "I just . . . felt like I should have wanted to. But it was a mistake."

"No, it wasn't."

"Yes, it was!" Sherae sounds furious. "How could you do that to me? To *us*? You destroyed everything we had."

"You're crazy. I didn't destroy anything. You're the one who walked away. We could get back together right now. We don't have to do anything if you don't want."

"It doesn't work that way. You can't go back to just making out once you've had sex. It becomes this thing that's expected."

"I won't expect it."

"Yes, you will. That's how you're wired."

"Sex is part of a relationship. It's what you do."

"Are you really that delusional? Not everyone is having sex."

"Well, they should be." I see Hector smiling in the side mirror.

"You're disgusting. I can't believe I was such an idiot."

"Hey." Hector reaches out to her. "I'm only joking."

"It's not funny." Sherae backs away from him. "You weren't listening to me that night, but I seriously hope you hear me now. Stop calling me. Stop texting me. Stop writing me notes. We were done the second you chose being a dumbass over being with me."

Sherae gets back in the car.

And we move forward.

eighteen

tuesday, may 10

(28 days left)

The toilet's not working again.

You'd think that mother would ask the landlord to call the plumber. Or to replace this ancient toilet so I could stop worrying every time I flush it. But mother refuses to tell the landlord that our toilet stopped flushing. She hasn't paid the rent for May yet. Calling the landlord would draw attention to that. I'm sure the landlord would be up here demanding the rent right now if she could actually climb the stairs to our place.

Last time this happened, the toilet stayed broken for a week.

Of course the busted toilet is the one in my bathroom. I have to be really quiet going through mother's room to get to hers so I don't wake her up. I slowly turn the doorknob. It makes a few small clicking sounds. Nothing drastic. I push the door open and peer into the darkness of her room, trying to see if she's awake.

Her curtains won't allow even one speck of sunlight to enter.

As I sneak past her bed, she remains an immobile lump under the covers. I'm sure she'd rather have me pee in a cup than wake her. I won't pretend I haven't considered that option.

◆　◆　◆

"Noelle, can you stay a minute?" Ms. Scofield asks at the end of class.

A jolt of fear stabs me. Why would she want to talk to me? I don't think I did anything wrong. The homework I handed in yesterday wasn't a masterpiece, but compared to everyone else's lame end-of-the-year attempts, I'm sure it was decent enough.

After everyone leaves, she waves me over to the desk in front of hers. "You have English now, right?"

"Yeah." How does she know my schedule? I don't think I've ever told her what I have next.

"I'll give you a pass. I don't have second period, so I thought this would be a good time to talk." Ms. Scofield picks up the prism she used with the spectrometer in today's demo. "Did you like the demo?"

I nod. "It was cool."

"Dusted off an oldie! So. How's everything going?"

If Ms. Scofield were any other teacher, I'd just say I'm fine and get my late pass. But she's Ms. Scofield. I can tell she's asking because she cares.

"It's been better," I admit.

"When?"

"What?"

"When was it better? Isn't high school a constant state of emotional turmoil?"

"Pretty much."

"Worst time *ever*. But it won't always be like this. I know that doesn't help much right now, but it's something to hold on to. If I'd stopped believing that my life would eventually get better, I don't think I would have survived high school."

"Seriously?"

"Absolutely."

"But you're so happy."

"I'm happy *now*. I was really depressed back then."

Ms. Scofield is kind of blowing my mind. I always assumed she was a shiny happy cheerleader type back in the day. She's always in a good mood. She's always smiling. Even when she got sick a while ago, she was still in high-energy mode. And now she's telling me she was depressed in high school? How is that even possible?

"What's your secret?" I ask.

She smiles. "I've already lived through the worst time of my life. So I know that whatever happens to me from now on, nothing will ever be as bad as it was back then. That makes me happy."

Ms. Scofield is a fellow survivor.

"Is that why you're so perky in the morning?" I ask.

"Partially. Also because I believe that everyone deserves a quality education. That motivates me to bring the energy."

"Oh, you bring it."

"I wish things were easier for you, Noelle. But all of the pain you're feeing right now will make you stronger. Trust me: that strength will make you a better person. Then you can help other people who aren't as strong."

"It's hard."

"I know it is."

Ms. Scofield would be an awesome mom. Too bad she doesn't have kids. She's not even married. I forget how it came up, but someone was asking about her family in class a while ago. She said that she wants to get married. She just hasn't found the right guy yet. She wants to have kids, too.

It's so wrong. Women who shouldn't be mothers can just go ahead and have kids like it's nothing. But some women who *would* be good moms don't have kids because they haven't found the right person to have them with.

How messed up is that?

"Did you hear about the paintball thing?" I ask. "Is that why you wanted to talk to me?"

"I did hear something about that."

The last thing I want to do is talk about what happened. I don't know if Ms. Scofield is expecting me to come right out and tell her. Part of me really wants to. It's just too hard.

"If you feel like talking, you know I'm here, right?"

I nod.

"I know you've been hurting lately. So I just wanted to let you know I'm always here."

Even if I don't talk to Ms. Scofield about everything, it's good to know I can.

nineteen

Ali Walsh killed herself last night.

twenty

wednesday, may 11

(27 days left)

I can't believe it. I was just talking to Ali yesterday. She asked me to explain one of the homework problems she didn't get.

And now she's . . . gone.

No one can figure out why she did it. No one has heard about anything horrible that might have pushed her over the edge. She even seemed happy when I talked to her in class.

I should have been there when she reached out to me.

I should have become better friends with her.

I should have done a lot of things that I'll never get another chance to do.

Counselors are such a joke. They expect you to tell them things you can't even tell yourself. They think that just because a girl who went here killed herself, we're all sad. Don't they realize that these kids made Ali's life miserable?

"Does anyone have something they'd like to share?" Mrs. Henley asks.

When I got to physics and saw Ms. Scofield, I could tell she was shattered over Ali. I almost went up to her. But Mrs. Henley was hovering nearby. All I know about Mrs. Henley is that she's the social worker. Which supposedly means she deals with tougher issues that regular guidance counselors aren't equipped to handle. We had to put our desks in a sloppy circle so we could all see each other. Mrs. Henley started by saying a bunch of stuff about loss and anger and how important it is to let your feelings out. I wasn't really listening.

Now she wants to know if anyone feels like sharing.

Here's the truth she doesn't want to hear:

People avoided Ali. No one knew her well enough to be grieving right now. They don't have the right to be sad. And P.S.? Mrs. Henley can't just chuck us in a circle and expect everyone to suddenly open up in front of people they would never talk to. That's just not the way it works.

"I know it's hard," Mrs. Henley says, "but this is a safe space. You can talk about anything that's on your mind."

Hilarious. The woman is beyond clueless.

Jolene DelMonico raises her hand. Mrs. Henley nods at her encouragingly.

"I think what happened was tragic," Jolene says. "Ali was *so* nice." Jolene sniffs loudly. She digs a pack of tissues out of her bag. "I just wish we could have done something to help her."

Bitch, please. Like you even knew her.

"It's natural to want to blame yourself," Mrs. Henley says in what is supposed to be a soothing tone but is actually grating on my nerves. "But this was no one's fault. There's nothing anyone could have done."

Someone snorts loudly.

Everyone looks at me.

Oh. I guess I was the snorter.

"Is there something you want to say?" Mrs. Henley asks me.

Why, yes, there is.

I want to say that there were lots of things we could have done.

I want to say that I hate how everyone's talking about Ali like they knew her.

I want to say that bullies shouldn't be allowed to destroy people's lives.

Most of all, I want to yell at myself for being so afraid. No one tried to stop Carly. If there's anyone who understood how it made Ali feel, it was me. But I didn't try to stop Carly, either.

I don't say any of those things. I just stay quiet and shake my head at the floor.

This is like what happened to Tyler. He was a boy in college who killed himself. It was all over the news. Tyler's roommate hid a webcam in their dorm room and streamed him in bed with another boy. The next night, Tyler jumped off the George Washington Bridge.

Carly and Warner and those guys make me wish I were dead all the time. I totally understand why Ali wanted to make everything stop. Being tormented day after day after relentless freaking *day* weighs on you. After a while, that weight becomes too much to carry. Ali needed a way out. So she took the only one she could see.

Ali was like me in so many ways. We were both careful not to let our secret agony show, even when we were screaming inside. Why didn't I do something to let her know she's not alone? That she *wasn't* alone. I wish I'd told her about The Road. About how it can lead to a better life if we keep holding on. If she had just held on a little longer . . .

I don't know how I'll ever stop hating myself.

◆   ◆   ◆

FACTS

Fact #1   *Mean people suck.*
Fact #2   *Bad things happen to good people.*
Fact #3   *Good doesn't always prevail over evil.*

◆   ◆   ◆

I was hoping that mother would be in one of her sulky moods at dinner. The last thing I wanted to hear tonight was a tirade. So of course she's on one of her worst negativity benders ever.

"These people have a serious problem with reading," she's complaining. "There's a sign right above the counter that says 'no refunds will be issued without a receipt.' So, you know, I'm trying to keep it together. I say, 'There's a sign right above you that says you need a receipt to get a refund, ma'am.' But she keeps insisting on a refund. You'd think I was speaking another language. So I explain our exchange policy . . ."

I can't eat. Not that a boiled hot dog and a lump of revolting potato salad is remotely appetizing.

Ten years later, mother takes a breath and actually glances in my general direction.

"You're not eating," she says.

I stare at my plate.

"You should eat," she says.

"Ali Walsh killed herself."

"Who?"

"A girl at my school."

"Oh, right. I heard about that."

"You did? Where?"

"At work. There was something about it on the news."

Seriously? Mother knew about Ali and she didn't even mention it? And she just spent all this time ranting about her own problems? How could she hear something like that and not even ask if I'm okay?

"Then why didn't you say anything?" I ask.

"To who?"

"To *me*."

"Why, was she a friend of yours?"

"You really don't get it, do you? How can you be that insensitive?"

"You shouldn't talk to your mother that way."

"You just spent the whole dinner complaining about work. You don't care that I have to sit here and listen to you spew every night about how horrible your life is. I might as well be this . . . busted candleholder! And how ridiculous is it to have candleholders on the table when you never even light any candles?!"

"I don't complain every night."

"All you ever *do* is complain! You never ask me about my day.

In case you haven't noticed, there are other people in the world. And their lives suck, too."

"Oh, really? Are those people single mothers trying to put food on the table and pay the rent in an expensive town? This isn't easy to do alone, for your information."

I suddenly realize that I'm shaking. I'm so furious I don't even know what to do. I want to throw her against the wall and bash her skull in.

"You act like you're the only single mother in the world. There are lots of single moms who are actually doing what they're supposed to. Just because you're alone doesn't give you an excuse to neglect your kid."

"How am I neglecting you?"

"Seriously?" I bolt out of my chair so fast it tips over. I'm shaking even harder. "You never talk to me about anything besides how much you hate your life. You keep telling me that I'm the reason you're so miserable. You don't even look at me. You don't get me the things I need. There's never anything to eat—look at this!" I go over to the refrigerator and yank it open. "There's nothing in here. Do you realize I have to make mayonnaise and mustard sandwiches for lunch? Do you have any idea how *humiliating* that is?"

"I don't have to listen to this."

"No, you *do* have to listen! You never showed me how to do laundry. You yell at me for normal stuff like turning the heat up or eating the rest of the cereal. You don't even let me take a freaking *shower* in the morning. *How can you not know how disgusting that is?!*"

Mother's eyes pierce mine. The sudden eye contact is a searing shock to my system. My heart is racing. I'm shaking so hard I'm sure she can see it. Good. I want her to see how upset she's making me.

"It's perfectly acceptable to take showers at night," mother says in her Scary Voice. Her Scary Voice is really quiet and trembly with an undercurrent of rage. "You're making me sound like some kind of monster. You have a roof over your head and food on the table. If you don't want to eat it, that's not my problem." She looks at me with disgust. "I made dinner after a long day at work and you didn't even bother to eat it. And now you're complaining that there's nothing to eat?"

This could be the night I finally lose it. Mother may have driven me officially insane. But if I get medieval on her ass, then I'll look like the crackpot and she'll look like the lucid one.

I stomp to my room and slam the door. Trying to make her understand is useless. She wants to keep living in her own delusional world and there's nothing I can do about it.

There should seriously be prerequisites for being a parent.

◆　◆　◆

I reach way back on the top shelf of my closet behind the blankets, grab my secret box, and lift it out. This is the first time I've taken the box out in over a year.

There was a time when I felt like I couldn't hold on anymore. So I put some things in this box and hid it. I wanted to be ready if I had to let go.

It would be so easy to escape like Ali did. Then maybe mother would care. Maybe everyone would.

But I can't do that. Because Ali could have been me. Ali saved me. She woke me up. She did the unspeakable thing I've been thinking about doing for so long. I owe it to her to keep living. I have to hold on to this life and never let go. I have to do it for Ali. I have to do it for myself.

Because I am DONE.

I am done being afraid to say the things that need to be said.

I am done letting a bunch of idiots I won't ever see again after next year affect my emotions.

I am done being humiliated by things that aren't my fault.

I am done feeling like I can't do anything to improve my life.

My life is happening right now. And whether it remains a complete disaster or starts getting better is up to me. I can't control everything, but there are some things I can change.

We're products of our choices. I can make a choice to do more than just survive. Which is why I'm going to start shaping my life into the one I want.

twenty-one

monday, may 30

(14 days left)

Sherae has taken over.

It started right after I told her the truth about my home life a few weeks ago. One of her new things is to pick up me and my laundry bag, take us to school, and then take us to her house after to do laundry. The dryer isn't drying anymore and mother refuses to tell the landlord about it. We're on our way to school, singing along to the radio.

This is the first good day I've had since Ali died. I wasn't expecting to be anywhere near okay again for a really long time. It felt like I was underwater and everything above the surface was distorted. I went to the movies with Sherae, but I couldn't really concentrate on the dialogue. All I could hear were these dark thoughts that wouldn't leave me alone. I couldn't stop obsessing over what I could have done to help Ali. But then I started throwing myself into my artwork. I made three new mobiles in a week. One of them has intricate spirals that took forever.

Emerging from my depression makes me feel guilty. But something tells me Ali would approve.

Every time I saw Carly, I threw her a cold glare, almost daring her to come up to me. But for some reason she didn't.

Sherae turns the volume down.

"I know, I suck at this part," I say. "You can turn it back up, though—I promise to shut up."

"It's not that. We need to fix the Julian situation."

"Sorry, did you not get the memo? There *is* no Julian situation."

"But there should be. It's ridiculous that you've been keeping yourself from him."

"I have my reasons."

"I'm declaring your reasons to be invalid." Sherae clicks her blinker to turn onto the road to school. "You don't want him to get too close because you're afraid he's not going to like you anymore, right?"

"Something like that."

"So we can change the things you think he won't like about you. Okay, we can't trade your mom in for a working one or get you a nicer home, but Julian's not going to care about those things. Trust me. And everything else is fixable."

"Really?"

"Absolutely! Did I not say I was taking over?"

"You did say that, yes."

"Well, this is me taking over. There's no reason you can't be with Julian. After school we're going to go to my house, start your laundry, and make a list of what we need to do."

I should explain to Sherae why it's too late for me and Julian. But I don't. I just sit back for the rest of the ride with the warm wind all around me. It's nice to be taken care of for a change.

◆　◆　◆

"Nice essay," Simon compliments me.

"Thanks."

Simon rolls his chair over to my desk. "No, I mean . . . this is really good."

When I joined lit mag, I told Simon that I wasn't going to write anything for it. But Ali inspired me. This essay for lit mag is my way of helping people understand why some kids commit suicide.

"Mr. Gilford is picking three of our writers to read their pieces to some English classes," he says. "I'm going to recommend you."

"What?"

"As much as I hate to admit it, not everyone reads the *Spectrum*. This would be a way for you to get your message out. What do you think?"

"I guess that would be cool."

"Dude." Simon springs out of his chair. The chair zings across the room. "We need to think bigger. Do you know how many kids out there are tortured every day? And we only hear about a fraction of the suicide cases."

A breeze blows in through the big window. They let you open

the windows all the way down here on the first floor. The upstairs windows only open a crack. I guess they're afraid that if those windows opened any higher, we'd be jumping out of them.

I go over to the window and open it some more. The breeze is soft. It smells like trees mixed with something sweet. The weather has been amazing all week. School totally has that end-of-year vibe. I take a deep breath. Summer is in the air. Breathing is easier.

"What are you doing this summer?" Simon asks.

"Working. If I can find a job. I seriously need to save for college."

"Want to start a zine?"

"What kind of zine?"

"The kind that will reach out and bring people together."

"Uh, yeah, I think I could make some time for that."

"Should it be online or in print?"

"Definitely online. We'll reach way more people that way. And we could get contributors from all over the world!"

"What if we did both?" Simon suggests. "We could focus mainly on the website, but also print a few hundred copies."

"Sounds like a lot of work."

"Not really. Zines were all physical cut-and-paste back in the day. We could use the same technique to make ours authentic and then just scan the pages. That way, we could still keep it old-school."

We frantically begin planning our zine. We want it to help anyone who feels alone by connecting people from all over. If we can get the first issue ready by the time school starts, we can even distribute some paper copies here as an underground thing.

Then it hits me. "Okay, thinking even bigger . . . what if we distribute them outside of school? Even outside of town? That would spark more interest in the website."

"I like it."

"We could ask around in the city and see if anyone would stock it. Like in bookstores and coffeehouses and stuff. And we'll put our website right on the cover so people know where to go."

"You. Rule." Simon sticks his fist out for a pound. I give him an exploding pound with sound effects.

This summer is going to rock. I'll find a job. I'll work on the zine with Simon. And maybe I can find a way to start making things better now instead of waiting until later.

◆　◆　◆

Part of being done means that I have to say the things I've been too afraid to say. Even though I am beyond nervous, I'm waiting for Julian at his locker. I told Sherae I was ready to talk to him after getting charged up in lit mag. She immediately insisted that I come over tomorrow instead.

When Julian comes down the hall, I almost faint from emotional overload. I seriously doubt he'll want to hear what I need to say. He'll probably just keep ignoring me the way he has ever since he found out about Matt. But I have to try.

He does not look happy to see me.

"Hey." I move aside so he can open his locker. "I'm . . . I totally understand if you don't want to talk to me. But can we go somewhere? I have some things I need to tell you."

Julian is busy packing his bag. My bag is already packed. I ran to my locker right after precalc so I could get everything I needed and be ready to go in case Julian agrees to leave with me. Which is still highly doubtful.

"Like what kind of things?" he says.

"Like . . . how I'm really, really sorry. I shouldn't have pushed you away. I hate that I did. But there are reasons why and . . . I can't tell you everything, but I want to tell you most of it."

Julian shuts his locker. He slings his messenger bag over his shoulder. "Let's go," he says.

We walk through the emptying halls in silence.

Out in the student parking lot, we get in Julian's white Trans Am. The only reason I know it's a Trans Am is because I heard Julian talking about it with his friends once. It's this rare vintage find his dad bought from a collector.

No one says anything.

"Are . . . can we go somewhere?" I say.

"Let's talk here."

"Okay." Cars are pulling out all around us. People are looking in at us as they walk by. Simon passes by on my side and makes a discreet power fist. I try to hide my smile.

"What's so funny?" Julian asks.

"Nothing. Simon Bruckner was . . . I'm really sorry, Julian. If I could take back what I said to you, I would."

"Which part?"

"All the bad parts. Like when I said I couldn't be with you. Because . . ." I take a deep breath. "I really want to be with you.

It wasn't just because of Matt. There are some things in my life that I'm embarrassed about and I thought if you found out about them, you wouldn't like me anymore. And the only way I could think to hide them from you was to push you away. But I'm ready to take a chance."

"What are you embarrassed about?"

"So many things. Like how my family isn't exactly as rich as everyone else's around here."

"You thought I wouldn't like you because of that?"

I nod.

"Do you really think I'm that shallow?"

"What? No! You're not shallow at all. It's just . . . we come from two different worlds. I don't fit in here. You do, but I'm . . ."

"You're not like everyone else."

"Exactly."

"Has it ever occurred to you that's what I love about you?"

Wait. Did Julian Porter actually use the words *I*, *love*, and *you* in the same sentence?

"It is?" I ask.

Julian reaches out to hold my hand. "It totally is."

We sit there for a minute, just holding hands and staring at each other. Julian leans a little toward me.

Someone pounds on the hood. "Get a room!" they shout.

That cracks me up. No one's ever told me to get a room before.

Julian sits up straight, pulls his hand away, and stares out the windshield.

"I need some time," he says.

"Oh. Okay."

Of course he needs time. I get that. I just hope he still wants to be with me.

Love is never guaranteed. Love is a risk we take because we hope it will make us happy. And Julian Porter is definitely worth the risk.

twenty-two

friday, june 3

(10 days left)

Last night I had a dream that there was this enormous rainbow. The colors were brighter than any colors I'd ever seen before. The rainbow began outside my front door. I stood where it started and made a wish.

I know what this one means.

◆ ◆ ◆

Simon must have been really persuasive with Mr. Gilford. He picked three writers to read their *Spectrum* pieces to some English classes: me, Darby, and a senior. It's weird to be calling myself a writer. But I guess that's what I am. I actually like the whole writing thing now. I'm even thinking about how I could use writing as my career.

For the longest time, I thought teaching would be the best way to directly impact kids' lives. Now I'm realizing that there are way more possibilities. It's wild how unexpected experiences can shape your life in ways you never saw coming. I was just trying to get out of lunch and now look.

The first class we visit seems relieved to get a diversion from the teacher. None of us wanted to read first, so we rock-paper-scissored for it. I have to go second. As Darby reads, I try to calm down. People in the front row can probably see my paper trembling.

I try not to look at anyone while I wait for my turn. But then I see Tommy, fellow solitary cafeteria survivor. He sees me see him. We both look away quickly, just like we used to when our eyes accidentally met at lunch.

I remember why I'm doing this. My paper stops trembling.

When it's my turn to read, it's like I'm talking right to Tommy. But I don't want to draw attention to him or anything. So I keep my eyes on my paper. The piece I wrote is about how we all affect the people around us, whether or not we realize it. It's about how everything is connected. And how each one of us can influence the fate of others by our own actions.

I take a deep breath before reading the last part.

"Are you the person you wanted to be? Or are you someone you don't recognize anymore?"

I sneak a look at Tommy after I'm done.

He's smiling right at me.

◆　◆　◆

"I heard you killed it!" Simon reports when I get to lit mag.

"Don't believe the hype." I collapse on my chair. Reading something that intense is emotionally draining. I've already read to three classes. We have two more to go.

"You rocked." Simon rolls over to me in his wheely chair. "I'm proud of you."

"Aw."

"This summer is going to be awesome."

"I know." I seriously cannot wait. Ever since we started planning our zine, I've been obsessing over it.

"Dude, I totally forgot about lunch!" Simon springs up. "What are you in the mood for?"

"Since when do we have a choice?"

"No, I mean . . . just so I can figure out what to get."

"I thought you said you always get extra because you can never decide."

"Oh, right." Simon smoothes his skinny mint-green tie. "Totally."

"That's not why you buy extra lunch, is it?"

Simon keeps smoothing his tie. "Not really," he admits.

I've had a feeling for a while that Simon made up the whole I-always-get-extra-lunch story. When other people are working in here with us, they usually bring their own lunch.

"Why do you buy me lunch?" I ask.

"Well. I know you've been giving up your lunch period to work here. Everyone's hungry by lunch, right?"

"But—"

"No buts. Be right back."

I thought I was hiding the worst parts of my life, but some things are just impossible to hide. Simon's probably heard my stomach growling in class. And I'm sure he's heard how Warner and those guys make fun of me. He just doesn't want to embarrass me by admitting he knows all that. Which means before I even realized it, Simon became one more person I could trust.

◆　◆　◆

This week has been excruciating. Waiting to find out if Julian still wants to be with me is the worst. Lingering after class every day. Willing the phone to ring every night. It's obvious Julian hates me. He's never going to talk to me again.

So why does it look like he's coming over to my locker?

This is the part where Julian tells me we're done.

"Hey," he says.

I can't talk to him. If I talk to him, then he will talk back. And what he'll talk about is how he never wants to talk to me again.

I shove my notebook in my bag. Or I'm trying to. It's not going.

"Here." Julian untangles the frayed lining of my bag from a notebook spiral.

"Thanks."

"Do you want to go to the city tonight?"

"What?"

"The city? The place with all the buildings?"

"Uh. Yeah. Of course."

"Sweet. I'll pick you up at seven?"

"Okay," I agree in a daze.

Maybe this is the part where my life gets good.

◆　◆　◆

Could I possibly be more stoked for tonight?

No. No, I could not possibly be.

Julian is taking me to the city. On our first date. Aka the Most Epic Date Ever.

Sherae insisted that I come over so we could figure out what I'm wearing. She filled a big shopping bag with clothes I can borrow. I majorly owe her for that. I mean, it's the city. I have to rock an actual look. Somehow I pulled off getting ready in time. I might even look halfway decent.

I still don't feel 100 percent over Matt, but I know it's time to move on. Matt was never the kind of boyfriend I wanted him to be. Deep down, I sort of knew it all along. I just didn't want it to be true.

Mother's not home yet. I leave her a note saying that I'm going to the movies with Sherae. Sherae is on board with this plan in the highly unlikely event that mother calls her.

There was no way I was letting Julian pick me up at home. I told him I'd meet him on the corner a few blocks away. Which is why I'm loitering on the sidewalk in front of the big house with pretty window boxes. Their yard has lots of purple flowers. The air smells like purple.

Julian's car pulls up. I remind myself not to slam the door

when I get in. Mother's old VW is so busted that you have to slam the door really hard on the passenger side. So I'm always slamming other people's car doors harder than I should.

I can't imagine ever fitting into Julian's world. It's hard to believe that he wants me there. But I want to trust him. At least, I want to try.

"Ready?" Julian says.

"Totally."

He pulls away from the curb. I don't know what music is playing, but I already like it.

"So . . . where are we going?" I ask.

"To the city."

"I know, but where are we going when we get there?"

"It's a surprise."

"Really?"

Julian nods. "You'll love it."

"Do I get a hint?"

"Nope." Julian turns the music up a notch. "Just sit back and enjoy the ride."

"I like this song."

"You know Bright Eyes?"

"No."

"Stick with me and you will."

I never knew you could have so much fun just riding in a boy's car. It's already the best time ever and we haven't even gone anywhere yet. When we get to The Road, it's way more exciting than the other times I've been on it. With the music playing and windows down and streetlights zipping by, that familiar rush of driving into the night hits me harder than ever.

I sneak looks at Julian. I like the way he taps his wheel to the music. Talking with him is really easy. I was worried that we'd run out of things to talk about. But we're discussing music and shows and art and architecture and just everything.

Every time we pass an exit, I imagine all of the places out there where I could live. There are so many places to set up a new life, so many different ways to be in this world. How do you know which one to choose?

When we get to the city, Julian finds a parking garage. I silently freak over how expensive it is. Julian is unfazed.

We walk to a cool coffeehouse called Nightfloat, where all these kids are hanging out. Some of them are definitely older, like in college, but some of them are our age. Everyone has their own original style. Not like back home where everyone wears the same standard outfits. The kids here look like they're having deep conversations about meaningful things.

"What can I get you?" Julian asks.

"Oh, I can—" I take my wallet out of my bag.

"No way. It's on me."

"Well, thanks. I'll have a coffee. Decaf."

"What size?"

"Small." I'm too nervous to deal with anything bigger.

"Find us a table?"

"I'll try." The place is packed. I manage to score us a little table against the wall right when two other kids are leaving.

I sit down. I try to relax. I can't decide what to do with my hands.

The more I look around, the more I get the feeling that this is a coffeehouse where the stranger you are, the more you fit in. Just the way I imagined the alternate universe would be. Nightfloat is obviously a magnet for cool kids. The authentic kind of cool—being true to yourself regardless of how different you are or what anyone else thinks of you. Not the plastic suburban kind where cool is defined by blending in.

The people here get it. These fringe teens are perfect for the zine. How awesome would it be if Nightfloat let us put some copies out? They already have piles of free papers stacked on the windowsill.

Julian comes over with our drinks. I'm so nervous my hand shakes when I take my mug from him. Coffee spills on his arm.

"Sorry!" I jump up and grab some napkins at the back counter. Then I actually start wiping off his arm. Which of course makes me blush because now I'm like attacking his arm.

"No worries." He takes the napkins from me.

Our table is really small, so we have to scrunch in. I scoot my chair in some more. But then my legs are totally touching Julian's legs. I scoot back. But I don't want to scoot back too far because then he'll think I don't want to touch him. Which I totally do.

Sitting at a table has never been this complicated.

"Cool place," I say.

"I'm glad you like it. It's charged and laid back at the same time, you know?"

"I was just thinking that."

Julian leans over the table. "Check out that guy's hat," he says quietly.

I blow on my coffee and look casually around first. Then I steal a look at the guy. He's wearing an electric-pink fedora with a bright red feather sticking out from the side.

"Awesome," I declare.

There's a bulletin board near the hat guy. It has a big poster for Mummenschanz.

"I love Mummenschanz!" I yell.

A girl at the next table with heavy glitter eye shadow and a lip ring smiles at me. "They rock," she confirms.

It's nice to be around people who are culturally aware enough to know what Mummenschanz is.

"What's Mummenschanz?" Julian asks.

"Only the best performance art troupe in the world. They dress up as these weird shapes, like a big cellophane sheet or a mouth, and they . . . just the way they move and everything conveys all this emotion without even speaking."

"Sounds interesting."

"They are. My favorite one is probably the tube. It's this big, yellow tube moving around—someone's inside it, but you can't see them—and there's a huge orange balloon that the tube keeps trying to grab. And then he pushes the balloon out to the audience—"

"Wait. Were they on *The Muppet Show*?"

"Yes! A really long time ago!"

"Dude, I saw them online! They're outrageous!"

"I know!"

"Those big, green lips—"

"—with the tongue!"

"Exactly!"

How amazing is this? No one ever knows Mummenschanz. But Julian does. And his leg is touching my leg.

He's not moving his leg away.

I'm not moving mine, either.

"So," Julian says. "What do you want to be?"

"Like, in general, or . . . ?"

"In life."

"I'm thinking of doing something with writing. Or teaching."

"What subject?"

"I'm not sure. You want to be an architect, right?"

"You remember that?"

"Of course. Your designs are unreal."

"Wow. Thanks."

"Your houses are like . . . they're all so different, but they all feel like home. I can totally imagine living in one of them. I can't wait to have my own home and fill it with pretty things."

Okay, what am I even saying? *Fill it with pretty things?* I sound like such a girl. But Julian doesn't seem bothered. We end up talking for what feels like ten minutes but is actually two hours.

"I can't believe it's this late already," I say, then immediately wish I could take it back. It makes me sound like I never go anywhere. Which I don't, but Julian doesn't have to know that.

"Come on," he says. "I want to show you something."

I know we should be getting home. But I really don't care. On the way out, I take a card so I can call the manager about stocking our zine.

We walk a few blocks to the mystery destination. Julian won't tell me where we're going. I wish we lived here. I'd have to adjust to the noise, though. I'm used to nothing but crickets and quiet. City sounds are all incessant traffic and a million voices and random bursts of music. Even some of the buildings have their own sound, like a humming.

I want to stay out all night. I wish we never had to go back.

"Don't look over here," Julian tells me after we cross the street. "Look over there."

"But I can't see where I'm going."

"Don't worry." Julian holds my hand. "I've got you."

Keeping my head turned to the side, I let Julian guide me the rest of the way.

"We're here," he says. "You can look."

At first I think he's talking about the office building we're in front of. I can't figure out why he'd bring me here. I mean, it's a nice building with its glossy black glass and window walls of light, but . . .

Then I see it. Outside the main entrance between two sets of benches. It's Brancusi's *Bird in Space*. Except it can't be the real one. It has to be a replica.

"How did you know this was here?" I ask.

"I didn't. I had to do some research."

We go over. I'm mesmerized by how real it looks. The shiny bronze surface. The distinct curvature. The way it looks like it's in motion even though it's standing still. It's all here. I could be looking at the real sculpture and not even know the difference.

I reach out to touch it, then pull my hand back.

"Go ahead," he says.

So I do. I run my fingers down the curved side. The bronze is cool and smooth.

"This is incredible," I say. "I can't believe you found it for me."

"I'd do anything for you. Don't you know that by now?"

And then.

Julian kisses me.

I kiss him back. His lips are soft. Way softer than I thought they'd be.

We're totally making out on the street in the city. Like people who live their lives with no regrets. It's even more intense than all those times I imagined.

I have to step back and look at Julian to convince myself this is actually happening.

"I know things are rough for you," Julian says. "I hate the way those morons treat you at school." He brushes some hair away from my face that's fallen out of its little clip. "I want to protect you from all that."

"I don't think you can."

"Let me try. Let me be the one you can count on."

I know I'm taking a massive risk with Julian. He could end up breaking my heart just like I was always afraid he would. But maybe not. Maybe he really means what he says.

It's time to take a big leap and hope he'll be there to catch me.

twenty-three

monday, june 6

(9 days left)

The only thing I could think about all weekend was kissing Julian. The second I wake up, I think about kissing Julian. Getting ready for school, I think about kissing Julian. I even catch myself smiling as I'm waiting for the bus, feeling Julian's arms around me, remembering how it felt when his lips were finally on mine.

Jasmine gives me a weird look on the bus.

"What's with you?" she asks.

"What do you mean?"

"You're smiling. You never smile."

"That's because I never had any reason to smile."

"Until now."

"Exactly."

"What's his name?"

"Who?"

"The boy who's making you smile."

"How do you know there's a boy?"

"Please," Jasmine says. "Just because I'm in sixth grade doesn't mean I'm stupid."

"Julian. His name is Julian."

"Sexy name. I approve."

I let myself be taken to school in a daze. The combination of lack of sleep and raging hormones is making me light-headed. If I have any hope of focusing today, I have to stop thinking about the kissing. Plus, I heard that every time you access a memory, you rewrite it a little bit. So our memories change over time. This is one memory I want to keep intact for as long as I can.

♦ ♦ ♦

Ms. Scofield asks me to stay after class. I can tell by her face that something's up.

"Mrs. Henley wants your mom to come in for a conference," she tells me.

"Why?"

"Remember when she was here for grief counseling? She was concerned that you were keeping too much anger in."

Mrs. Henley could tell I was angry? I didn't think it showed.

"And right before that counseling session, Mrs. Henley heard about your bruises from the nurse."

"My mother doesn't hit me or anything. Those were from paintballs."

"The nurse said she asked you who shot the paintballs, but you wouldn't tell her."

"It gets worse if you tell."

Ms. Scofield sighs. "I know exactly what you mean. But no one should get away with doing that to you."

"So why does she want my mother to come in?"

"We're all . . . we're concerned about you. We just need to talk to her."

"How do you know all this?"

"Because I care about you, Noelle."

My throat gets tight. It's really hard not to cry.

When I get to Mrs. Henley's office, mother is waiting on the bench outside. Now that I have to deal with her being here, crying seems like a definite possibility.

"Do you know why they called me?" mother asks my shirt.

"Not really."

"It's highly disturbing to get a call at work asking me to come to your school, you know?"

"Not really."

She shifts her gaze closer to my face. "What?"

"I don't really know what that's like, no."

"Why are you—"

"Ms. Wexler?" Mrs. Henley comes out of her office, smiling and extending her hand to mother. "I'm Robin Henley. Hi, Noelle."

"Hi," I say.

Mother is not smiling back. She says, "I'm sorry, you're . . . the social worker?"

"Yes."

"I didn't know they had one of those."

"They do. Shall we?" Mrs. Henley waves us in. I didn't really notice Mrs. Henley when she did her grief counseling thing. She's pretty and her clothes are a lot nicer than teachers' clothes and her office is cheerful and welcoming. When I go in after her, Mrs. Henley touches my shoulder for a second. The hostility I felt toward her before has disappeared.

The mortification starts right away. Mother sits down in one of the two chairs across from Mrs. Henley's desk. And, I'm not even making this up, she says, "I'll just take my jacket off. Not that I'm warming up to you."

I turn away, wishing that when I look back mother will be gone. Where's the Normal Mom Act? How can she think being rude will help? Does she seriously want a social worker to know how damaged she is?

I try to tell Mrs. Henley how sorry I am with my eyes.

She gives me a reassuring look. Then she says, "Actually, Noelle, would you mind waiting outside? I'll call you back in soon."

Out on the bench, I put my feet up and pull my legs in close, resting my chin on my knees. I can hear some kids laughing in the classroom across the hall. A boy gets a drink at the water fountain. The fluorescent light above me buzzes.

Then I hear mother yelling, "How dare you accuse me of neglecting my daughter!"

My stomach lurches. I'm sure mother thinks this is all my fault. She probably thinks I went to Mrs. Henley and told her everything. As if I really want mother anywhere near this place. And

I definitely don't want all the teachers gossiping about me. Teachers would never admit that they gossip about students, but they totally do.

When Mrs. Henley comes out to get me, the last thing I want to do is go back in. But of course there's no choice. I don't even have to look at mother to absorb how mad she is. She's giving off vibes so toxic I'm worried that Mrs. Henley's bamboo plant will wither and die.

"We're concerned about you, Noelle," Mrs. Henley says. "We won't tolerate bullying. We need to know who hit you with those paintballs so we can help you."

Mrs. Henley seems like a sweet person. I believe her when she says she wants to help. Part of me even wants to sit back and let her take care of me. But there's no way she can understand what goes on for real. Which seems to be a common problem among grownups.

I stay quiet.

"Can you please explain to Mrs. Henley here that I feed you?" mother says in her Scary Voice.

"Huh?"

"I feed you, right? You're not malnourished or anything? Apparently, the nurse thinks you're malnourished."

Is she really that stupid? Of course I'm malnourished. I'm always trying to hide in oversized shirts and stuff. Except I have been wearing new tees that fit lately. And the nurse did see the way my ribs stuck out when I lifted my shirt.

Mother sighs dramatically. "Will you tell her?"

If I admit how horrible mother is in front of Mrs. Henley, she could get in a lot of trouble. Sherae said they could even take me away from her. Which sounded awesome at first. But I'd have to live in some foster home with strangers, which would be hideous. As bad as living with mother is, there are worse things. And there's only one more year left before I leave for college. So I'd rather not say anything.

But. I remember my promise to be done. Being done means not hiding anymore. It means not letting fear or shame dictate my decisions. Maybe if I told the truth in front of someone other than mother, she'd emerge from the delusional world she lives in.

"No," I say. "I mean, yes. I mean . . . there's not enough to eat. There's never enough to eat. Don't pretend like you don't know."

If I'd just slapped her, mother would be less shocked.

"Of course there's enough to eat," she contends. "Don't be ridiculous. I put dinner on the table every night."

"Hot dogs and frozen fries don't count as real food. And when the only thing I can make for lunch is a mayonnaise and mustard sandwich—if I'm lucky—that's a problem." My face immediately gets hot. It is mortifying to admit that in front of someone like Mrs. Henley.

"Hey, kid," mother says. "We're eating. That's real enough." Mother rolls her eyes at Mrs. Henley. "She doesn't understand how hard it is for single mothers." As if Mrs. Henley would ever be on her side. Doesn't mother realize how deranged she sounds?

I lock eyes with Mrs. Henley. She truly sees me. Whatever happens next, I have to believe that it's the right thing. I have to trust that there are people in my life who actually care about me.

And I have to let them help.

◆ ◆ ◆

I'm alone in the lit mag office when Sherae comes in. "How'd it go with your mom?" she says.

"How'd you get out of class?"

She holds up her hall pass. "I have like five minutes. What happened?"

I tell her everything.

"Oh my god," she says. "Your mom is unbelievable. It's like nothing ever fazes that woman."

"I know. You should have heard her with the whole warming-up-to-you thing. I was *mortified*."

"Did Mrs. Henley say if she's going to do anything?"

"She wants me to come in for counseling twice a week next year. And she told my mother she was going to follow up with her, but I'm not sure what that means. I could tell Mrs. Henley was not a happy unit. I'd really like to know what they were talking about when I wasn't in there."

"She probably told your mom she needs to shape up or she'll get in trouble. Remember those kids who were so starved they snuck out at night and scavenged food from their neighbors' garbage cans?"

"I'm not exactly eating out of the garbage."

"You know you can come over for dinner any night you want, right?"

"Or I could just move in. Your mom would totally adopt me."

"Totally."

Sherae has also been in to see Mrs. Henley. It took her a while after the whole parking lot confrontation with Hector. But she eventually told Mrs. Henley everything. Mrs. Henley assured Sherae that she's not alone. Lots of girls feel like having sex before they're ready is something they have to do to keep their boyfriends. Or that it's what everyone does. But about half of teen girls are virgins. Mrs. Henley explained that any time you have sex when you don't want to, it's not okay. Even if you're in a relationship. Even if it's someone you love.

Mrs. Henley was proud of Sherae for coming to her. She said that most girls never report attempted rape or even rape. They're usually too embarrassed to speak up. Which is really sad. The boys who took advantage of them should be the embarrassed ones.

"Oh, I almost forgot." Sherae takes our latest cootie catcher out of her back pocket and holds it out to me. "Here."

I take it from her. It's almost finished. After I finish this one, it will officially be our last cootie catcher of the year. I think I'll make the fortunes extra hopeful this time.

Simon comes in, carrying a box.

"Is this an authorized visitor?" he jokes. Ever since the Carly attack, he's been super protective. He only leaves me alone in here for a few minutes when he absolutely has to. But he knows Sherae.

"Sherae is always authorized," I confirm.

Sherae gasps at the clock. "You guys, I am *so* dead. I've been gone for fifteen minutes. There's no way I can explain that."

"Yeah, no, that's not good," Simon agrees. "You should just stay here for the rest of class."

"You should. Do you really want everyone thinking you were in the bathroom this long?"

"It'll look even worse if I wait until class is over."

"No, it won't," I say. "If you go in after the bell rings, everyone will forget you were gone. And anyone who sees you will know you were cutting. Trust me, I'm an expert on timing classroom entrances."

Sherae thinks it over. "Okay," she decides. "I'm staying."

"What's in the box?" I ask Simon.

"The *Spectrum*."

"Sweet!"

Simon grabs some scissors and slices the box open. I can't wait to see how they look.

The cover is gorgeous. It's a photo of a country road leading into the woods. The tone is all dreamy and nostalgic. It looks like the photo was taken right after a sun shower. There's the slightest hint of a rainbow in the distance. When I first started lit mag, Simon explained that every year the cover design has to incorporate a spectrum in some way.

"They look amazing," Sherae says. "Can I see one?"

"You can *have* one." Simon gives Sherae a copy. "Aren't you glad you're friends with the editors? You get yours a whole day before everyone else."

Sherae flips through the magazine until she finds my piece. She hugs me with one arm as she reads. This feeling builds up inside me like a balloon. I can't tell what it is at first. And then I realize that, maybe for the first time ever, I'm proud of myself.

No one should be ashamed to speak up. Shame makes it easy for neglect and abuse and bullying to stay huddled together in their dark corner. It's time to throw the switch on this spotlight. If I can inspire other kids to speak their truth, then everything I've been through will have been worth it.

◆　◆　◆

I'm getting stuff out of my locker for my last two classes when my radar detects Carly coming down the hall. A surge of Done rushes through me. I almost don't care if she attacks. She was in the last English class I read my lit mag piece to. Something about the way she was slouched in her seat smirking made me say, "This is dedicated to Ali Walsh" before I started reading.

Carly passes behind me. She says, "Good thing she killed herself. One less loser in the world."

"What?" I ask Carly's back. "I don't think I heard you."

She whirls around. "Hmm?"

"What did you just say?" I ask louder.

Carly gets right in my face. "I *said*. One less loser in the world."

"You're part of the reason she killed herself. Don't you get that? How can you go around trash-talking Ali when you're the one who pushed her over the edge?"

Shock flickers in Carly's eyes. She can't believe I'm calling her out. She even shrinks back for a second.

And then she lets loose.

"You think it matters that freak's gone? You really think anyone cares? Who cared when she was alive?"

"A lot of us! Me and her family and—"

"I had nothing to do with it. I didn't even do anything."

"Seriously? You tortured her every day. You've been harassing me since eighth grade. How do you think it feels to always be worrying about what you're going to do? Or what you're going to shout in front of everyone? And that thing with the paper cutter? You acted like it was some kind of game. That's just twisted."

There's rarely a big, explosive scene in the hall around here. So it's not surprising that everyone is staring at us. I even see Matt pushing up from the back of the crowd. The whole school will probably be talking about this by eighth period.

Good. Let them talk.

Carly shoves me, forcing me to take a step back. "You need to watch it," she warns.

I get right back up in her face. "No, *you* need to quit ruining other people's lives. What, shoving me makes you feel good? Does it make you feel good to beat up your little brothers, too?"

"I don't touch them! I'm the one who takes care of them! You act like you're the only one with problems."

"Yeah, we know you have problems, Carly," Matt drawls. "Like how your mom is a disgusting drunk."

Carly huffs off. I highly doubt that even having the most humiliating part of her life broadcast to the entire world will make her less obnoxious. She's not about to change. What has to change is how I let her affect me.

I deserve to be happy. I'm sad it took me so long to get that. But I get it now.

◆　◆　◆

TOP FIVE WAYS PEOPLE CAN SURPRISE YOU

5. Just when you think they've given up on you, they prove that they never will.
4. They find a way to speak up after staying silent for so long.
3. They defend you when you least expect it.
2. By showing you how life can get better now.
1. By helping you find a place to belong.

twenty-four

tuesday, june 7

(8 days left)

ꟻ had this realization about inertia. In physics, we learned that an object at rest remains at rest unless acted upon by an outside force. But now I realize that the force can come from inside. If you feel stuck, you have the power to unstick yourself. Although . . . when you think about it, the inner force I gained did come from outside forces. So I guess Newton was right after all.

The other part of Newton's First Law says that objects in motion remain in motion unless something comes along to change that. I feel like I might actually be in motion now. The good kind of motion, where you're moving forward. Where you refuse to let a bad day stop you. Where you're committed to keep going no matter what.

If I can just stay in motion, I think I'll be okay.

◆　◆　◆

When I get home from school, it takes me a second to realize what's going on.

Mother is bending over a pile of clothes in the middle of my room.

My clothes. From my closet. That are scattered on the floor with the rest of my stuff. She even dug out the stained white pants I shoved way in the back two years ago.

"What are you doing?" I panic.

I glance around for my secret box. It's sitting right there on the floor, out in the open for anyone to see.

"You went through my *stuff*?" I yell. "Who said you could do that?"

I wait for her to say something like, "I pay the rent. I can do whatever I want." But she doesn't have a snarky comeback for once.

Mother goes over to my secret box. She picks it up. I hate that she's touching it.

"What is this?" she says quietly.

"What do you think?"

She looks at me. Like, *really* looks at me. In my eyes. Which is seriously disturbing.

And then . . . she just bursts out crying.

I drop my bag. I don't know what to do. In normal families, I assume people comfort other people when they cry. But we don't know how to do that. So I kind of move a little closer to her and wait to hear why she violated The Fortress.

When mother calms down enough to talk, she says, "Mrs. Henley said you're at risk for being suicidal."

Mother was acting even stranger than usual last night. Clearly, Mrs. Henley freaked her out. I kept waiting for her to tell me what they talked about when I was sent out of the office. Of course mother couldn't just come out and tell me. She'd rather empty my entire closet than initiate a difficult conversation.

"I'm not suicidal," I say.

Mother lifts the lid off my secret box. She takes out a pack of razor blades, an X-Acto knife, and two boxes of sleeping pills.

"Then what's all this?"

"It's from a long time ago. I'm not going to do anything."

"But you *were* going to?"

We never talk like this. Ever. I used to wish that mother would have real talks with me, but now that one is happening I kind of want her to go back to ignoring me.

"Not really," I say.

She inspects a box of pills. "Where did you get these?"

"They're really old. They're probably expired."

"Why do you still have this stuff if you're not planning to use it?"

"I don't know." It's hard to explain. My secret box is symbolic. It's like I've been holding on to it to remind myself that things could be worse.

Mother starts crying again.

I have no idea what to do. I've never seen her like this. I can't believe she's crying because of me. But I think it's a good thing. Because it proves that, contrary to all evidence, mother might actually care.

twenty-five

wednesday, june 15

(a whole lifetime left)

"Everything you said about this place is true," Sherae raves.

We're at Nightfloat, that sweet coffeehouse in the city. It's me, Julian, Sherae, and Simon. Julian drove us here to celebrate the happy fact that summer vacay starts in two days.

"It's even better than I remembered," I marvel.

Simon gets up from the table we finally managed to snag. "Who wants what?" he asks. "My treat."

"Well, in *that* case . . ." Julian starts.

"Sherae and I want coffee cake," I say. I look at Sherae. We crack up.

"Is coffee cake like code for something?" Simon asks.

"You had to be there," Sherae explains.

"I wish I was," Simon tells her. He's all hovering by Sherae. Then he snaps out of it and goes up to the counter.

"Hey," Julian says. "I didn't get to order."

"Yeah, Simon's a little distracted at the moment." I've noticed that Simon seems increasingly distracted around Sherae. Not that Sherae's ready to notice any boy noticing her. But maybe she'll be ready next year. How awesome would it be if Simon and Sherae started going out?

A band has been setting up in the corner. Hipster boys on guitars strum chords. The badass girl drummer does a sound check. The lead singer's shaggy brown hair falls across his eyes as he reaches down to adjust some cables. He shakes his hair back and leans into the mic.

"Hey," he goes. "I'm Jordan. We're Residue. Let's rock."

Julian slides his chair closer to mine and puts his arm around me. Our legs are touching under the table. I press my leg against his. He presses back.

I love having the whole summer ahead of me, glimmering with possibility. I already have a summer job lined up at the bookstore. Plus, I'm hoping things at home will keep improving. Mother has been acting better ever since her breakdown. She still complains, but she's been making an effort to ask me about my life instead of just ranting about hers. She was even flexible when I talked to her about making some grocery shopping changes. I'm getting into cooking. I had no idea there were so many different kinds of salads until I started watching cooking shows. I have a special notebook where I write down recipes I want to try.

Mrs. Henley said something interesting in counseling the other day. We were talking about why fitting in is so important to me. The conversation drifted over to mother and her own issues about fitting in. I started thinking about what it must be like for mother to live in our town. Being the only poor parent in a rich area can't be easy. She must be really embarrassed, too.

Sometimes I look at pictures from when I was little, back when mother took care of me. In this one picture, I'm sitting on the floor by the big Christmas tree we always had when we lived with Lewis, opening a present. Mother's holding one of my pigtails and putting the elastic back on. I always looked at that picture and wondered, *Why did she stop taking care of me?* Now I think I understand.

Which doesn't mean I forgive her for neglecting me. Not at all. I just have to understand where she's coming from. I'm supposed to keep going to counseling all summer with a psychologist Mrs. Henley put me in touch with. She charges on a sliding scale, so I'll be going practically for free.

Of course, the best part of this summer will be Julian. I still can't believe I have a real boyfriend. Someone who sees the true me and likes what he sees. I love that he wants to take care of me. And now I'm ready to let him.

Julian leans in close. "I have something for you," he whispers.

"What is it?"

"We'll be right back," Julian tells Sherae and Simon. They're enraptured by Residue.

Julian takes me out into the warm almost-summer night. We

sit on a cute bench against the window. The bench sits between two trees with pink and white lights.

"I know you've been through a lot," Julian says. "I wish there was some way I could save you from all the badness. I just . . . want you to be happy."

"You *did* save me. And you always make me happy."

"But I wanted to do something monumental." Julian takes a folded piece of paper out of his back pocket. "I started this the night I got home from our first date. I was too pumped to sleep. Sorry it's wrinkled."

I unfold the paper. There's some kind of floor plan sketched out. I'm not sure what it's supposed to be.

"It's your dream home," Julian says. "I mean, I'm pretty sure it is. Based on everything you've told me. See, here's your enormous kitchen. That's the cooking island and here's where your Sub-Zero goes. And this"—Julian points to a smaller room next to a space labeled *Great Room*—"is your reading room. It's lit entirely by natural light—see the glass wall and the skylight? And it has a slanted ceiling for you to hang your mobiles."

I'm overwhelmed. Julian did this for me? He cares enough about me to know what my dream home would look like? And then to *design* it for me? He put in all the things I love, everything I've talked about having one day.

"This is . . . amazing." There's no way I could ever thank him enough. No one's ever done anything this incredible for me.

"I knew I wanted to do this when you said you couldn't wait to have a home and fill it with pretty things. If I could build this for you right now, I would."

Maybe Julian really will build my dream home one day. But for now, the place where I feel at home doesn't have to be a house. It can be any place I belong. Like in this city or with my friends . . . or just knowing that I belong right there in the moment, wherever I am.

There's a tap on the window behind us. Simon is waving us in.

"A toast!" Simon booms when we get back to our table.

We all hold our mugs up.

"To our zine that is yet to be named. May it help many people feel less alone. To new relationships. And to summer."

We all tap our mugs together.

Things are finally happening. It's time to dream even bigger.

I want our zine to unite teens all across America. I want everyone to be inspired by my words.

And this is what I'll tell them:

For kids stuck in small towns everywhere who feel like you'll never escape, I hear you. We are all connected. We're all in this together. You are not alone.

No matter what happens, never *ever* give up.

Happiness is not limited. There's enough for everyone. You can start right now, today, to move toward a happier life. Your life is shaped by your choices. Make ones that will help you get where you want to go.

Find your place to belong. It may not be a physical place. At least, not yet. Maybe your place is somewhere you let your imagination take you. Maybe it's your vision of the way your ideal life will be.

Eventually, you'll find a real place that feels like home. Your whole world will open up in ways you kept believing were possible. And you'll be so happy you held on long enough to make it there.

So let's do this thing. Let's own what makes us unique. Let's refuse to allow haters to stop us from moving forward. Let's turn our dreams into reality.

Starting now.

Dear Readers,

When I was a teen, I would have been mortified to admit that I was being bullied at school. My junior high and high school years were the worst time of my life. Kids picked on me for being a science nerd. They picked on me for not wearing the expensive sweaters and jeans everyone else had. They picked on me for doing weird things like writing song lyrics on my sneakers (this was back in the day before writing on your sneakers was cool). I was embarrassed by all the ways I didn't fit in.

I am not embarrassed anymore.

After I left for college, I realized that being weird is awesome. You have to stand out if you want to make a difference in the world. I couldn't believe I'd wasted so much time wishing I fit in with a bunch of people I'd probably never see again for the rest of my life. Suddenly, I was surrounded by hundreds of accepting people who rocked their unique qualities. My real life had finally started and I was determined to never look back again. Of course, writing teen novels involves looking back every day. But that's okay. Now that I can hopefully help you guys, enduring those bad times was worth it.

Surviving painful times builds strength. You can use that strength to help other people who are going through similar experiences. The torment I survived sparked an ambition to reach out and help other teens feel less alone. That sense of purpose motivated me to become a teacher. And now I connect with way more teens as an author. That's why I love my job.

I know what it's like when this life thing gets beyond exhausting. Some days it feels like you'll never be happy again. On your worst days, the days when it seems like everything is going wrong, when you want to hide from the world and never come out, please know this: I was in that dark place, too. And I made it to the other side. I created a life that makes me happy. If I could do it, so can you.

The most important thing I want to tell you is this: Never give up on your dreams. No matter how many people say it's impossible, no matter how difficult your journey is, you can create your ideal life. Your heart's desires can become reality. Make things better now by taking steps every day to get closer to the life you want.

And never, ever give up.

Love,
Susane

Resources for Readers

Whatever you're going through, please know that you are not alone. Friendly neighbors are out there who want to help you. Here are a few of them:

Above the Influence—abovetheinfluence.com
Being above the influence is about being yourself—and not letting people pressure you into being less than you. It's also about having positive influences in your life and knowing that you can be a positive influence on other people. You have the power to reject the negative influences that can bring you down, including the pressure to use drugs, pills, and alcohol.

To Write Love on Her Arms—twloha.com
To Write Love on Her Arms is a movement dedicated to presenting

hope and finding help for people struggling with depression, addiction, self-injury, and suicide. If you are worried that you or someone you know may be at risk for suicide, please call the National Suicide Prevention Lifeline at 1.800.SUICIDE.

A Thin Line—athinline.org

New issues like forced sexting, textual harassment, and cyberbullying have emerged, which now affect a majority of teens in the States. A Thin Line was developed to empower teens to identify, respond to, and stop the spread of digital abuse in their lives and among their friends. The campaign is built on the understanding that there's a "thin line" between what may begin as a harmless joke and something that could end up having a serious impact on you or someone else.

It Gets Better Project—itgetsbetter.org

The It Gets Better Project was created to show young LGBT people the levels of happiness, potential, and positivity their lives will reach—if they can just get through their teen years. The It Gets Better Project reminds teens in the LGBT community that they are not alone—and it *will* get better.

The Trevor Project—thetrevorproject.org

The Trevor Project is determined to end suicide among LGBTQ

youth by providing lifesaving and life-affirming resources including their nationwide, 24/7 crisis-intervention lifeline at 1.866.4.U.TREVOR.

Love Is Respect—loveisrespect.org

Love Is Respect is a joint project between the National Dating Abuse Helpline and Break the Cycle to provide resources for teens, parents, friends, and family. All communication is confidential and anonymous. The National Dating Abuse Helpline at 1.866.331.9474 is a national 24-hour resource that can be accessed by phone or the Internet, specifically designed for teens.

Rape, Abuse & Incest National Network (RAINN)—rainn.org

RAINN is the nation's largest anti–sexual assault organization. It operates the National Sexual Assault Hotline at 1.800.656.HOPE and the National Sexual Assault Online Hotline at rainn.org. The hotline's services are free and confidential. RAINN leads national efforts to prevent sexual assault, improve services to victims, and ensure that rapists are brought to justice.

Stay Teen—stayteen.org

The goal of Stay Teen is to encourage you to enjoy your teen years and avoid the responsibilities that come with too-early pregnancy and parenting. The more you know about issues like sex, relationships, waiting, and contraception, the better prepared you will be to make informed choices for your future.

Leave Out Violence (LOVE)—leaveoutviolence-us.org
Leave Out Violence was created to reduce and help eliminate violence in the lives of teens and their communities by initiating a movement of youth spokespeople who communicate a message of nonviolence.

Susane Colasanti Wants to Help You Create Your Ideal Life ...Starting Now.

Back in high school, I felt like my real life wouldn't begin until I left for college. The waiting was excruciating. But then I realized that my real life was already happening. And while there were lots of things I couldn't control, there were many changes I *could* make to improve my life.

Your Ideal Life is a presentation designed for teens of all ages. My goal is to motivate participants to identify their goals, then work toward achieving them. I want to inspire teens to turn their dreams into reality. Participants learn how they can improve their lives and the lives of those around them by maximizing positive energy. Working toward goals while trying to make the world a better place is a synergistic approach to creating a happy, productive life.

The presentation includes a workshop component. I guide

participants through the process of identifying what's most important to them, considering both short- and long-term goals. Everyone then develops a viable plan to take daily steps toward reaching the goal that is most important to them. All participants take away a tangible reminder of their heart's desires and ways to begin making them reality.

I believe that by focusing on the things that matter most to us every day, our thoughts, words, and actions will all be affected in positive ways that will help move us closer to achieving our goals. Your Ideal Life helps teens explore what they can do to improve their lives right now and encourages everyone to make positive choices that will shape both their present and future.

Teachers, librarians, school administrators, and conference coordinators may schedule a visit by contacting Susane at susanecolasanti.com.